AWAKEN THE ADVENTURE!

The Death Walkers are rising and
bringing plagues of evil to the world.
It's up to YOU to stop them!

1. Go to Scholastic.com/TombQuest

2. Log in to create your character
   and enter the tombs.

3. Have your book ready and enter
   the code below to play:

R4RRMFMCX7

Scholastic.com/TombQuest

Hieroglyphic Alphabet

TOMBQUEST

AMULET KEEPERS

MICHAEL NORTHROP

SCHOLASTIC INC.

For my brother, Matthew,
and the Dungeons & Dragons games
that never really end.
— M.N.

Library of Congress Control Number: 2014951451

ISBN 978-0-545-72339-8

10 9 8 7 6 5 4 3 2 1   15 16 17 18 19

Printed in the U.S.A.   23
First edition, May 2015

Book design by Keirsten Geise

Dead Man Walking

A large figure descended the steep slope of Swain's Lane in north London. The man's features were old, but his frame was strong and he moved in long, sure strides. Each step of his heavy, old boots brought him closer to the slumbering neighborhood below. The warm summer night was dark out here so far from the city's glittering center. The man brushed one heavy hand against the tall black fence posts as he passed.

Thick fingernails struck old iron: *Tik tik tik!*

On the other side lay a very old cemetery, built into the hillside. He looked in at the moss-shrouded grounds with ink-dark eyes: considering, remembering. The cemetery was mostly full now, had been since World War I. It was a sleepy place. Deathly quiet. *Tik tik tik!* He let his hand drop. The fence ended; the village began.

The man moved more quietly now, like a cat settling in for the hunt. The first little houses appeared, huddled close together, their windows dark. A few moments later, he saw light up ahead, movement. The faintest hint of a smile formed on his death-parched lips.

"Aw, don't eat that!" said Bennie Kemp, tugging on the leash. "Spitfire! Spitfire! Bad dog!"

The British bulldog looked back and, reluctantly, dropped the candy wrapper. *Empty anyway*, his little dog brain thought.

"Just do your business and let's go," said his owner. "Creepy out here."

Spitfire looked back blankly. He understood several words — *food, walk, biscuit* — but none of those.

Bennie looked around the streets of his little neighborhood. He was surprised how deserted they were. He'd heard the rumors, of course. Everyone had. But having been raised on tales of British bravery, he was a little disappointed in his neighbors. *A few people go missing and the whole town shuts down*, he thought. He could barely manage half a thought for the reports of blood falling from the sky and other mysterious events. He chalked that all up to public hysteria stoked by the media.

"Bunch o' nonsense," he said grouchily to Spitfire's back.

The dog didn't even bother to turn around this time. *Talk to me when you've got a biscuit.* Instead, he kept feverishly sniffing the ground with his blunt, slobber-covered snout. There was something dead up ahead, and he Had To Find It! Now he was the one tugging on the leash. It could be anything: a squirrel, a pigeon, a cat — oh, how he hoped it was a cat! He pulled his owner toward the smell.

As Bennie followed his lumpy little leader out of the glow of one streetlight and toward the glow of another, he saw a man. *It is a man, isn't it?* he thought. His face was creased with deep lines, but his body was large and solid. The combination reminded Bennie of a statue from a village green. The outfit, too. He looked like an explorer from the height of Britain's colonial might. *Dressed for the heat of India or Africa*, Bennie thought.

"You all right, then?" said Bennie. "Gave me a fright."

Spitfire finally peeled his stubby nose from the sidewalk. *Well, this is the dead thing*, he thought. *But it's all wrong.*

The man released a slow, ragged breath — air moving through damaged passageways like the hiss of old pipes — and then he looked up. Bennie got a better look at the man's skin now. Even in the faint light, he could see that it was horribly uneven, too leathery in some places, too loose in others. And then he saw the eyes.

Oh dear Lord, the eyes . . .

A scream pierced the night, followed by a few quick, sharp barks. One final yelp and the streets were silent again. And all around them, the houses were quiet, too. A bedside lamp clicked on and then quickly clicked off again. The rest of the windows remained dark. The neighbors stayed in their beds, pulling the sheets a little closer.

And so none of them saw the powerful figure of one man drag the limp frame of another out of the light at the edge of the village and up the long rise of Swain's Lane.

The rest of the night crept by without incident. Heavy eyes closed again, troubled minds found a few hours of rest, and a frightened bulldog huddled against a locked door. But the horrors were not quite over for the lonely dog's former owner.

Early the next morning, hidden from the freshly risen sun, an ancient ritual began. The residents woke from broken sleep and bad dreams to the sound of rain thumping on their roofs, spattering against their windowpanes. If there's one thing the English know, it's the sound of rain. And these drops were too thick, by the sound of them, to be mere water.

Night Flight

The big airliner flew through the night, and Alex Sennefer sat in the dark cabin and thought about the dead and the missing. The dead: the Death Walker he had put to rest back in New York, and the one he was almost certainly flying toward. The missing: his mom.

The plane would arrive in London early the next morning. Right now, it was somewhere over the vast, cold Atlantic Ocean. Alex drummed his fingers on his thigh, impatient, wanting to be there already, wanting to get started. He looked over at his best friend, Renata Duran. Ren was conked out in the window seat. She'd placed the cheap airline pillow against the wall and crumpled sideways into it. Her eyes were closed and her mouth was just slightly open, almost touching the little window. Alex looked through the safety glass, but all he saw was moonlight and a spiderweb of frost from the minus-eighty-degree temps outside. *How can she sleep with everything that's going on?* he thought. But he knew he should try to get some rest, too.

He took one last look up the aisle toward first class, where he was pretty sure his cousin Luke was already asleep. His cousin wasn't the type to stay up thinking. He honestly wasn't the type to think all that much while he was awake. Technically, he was headed to London to attend an elite track-and-field camp, but Alex was pretty sure he was also going to keep an official family eye on him. *What's left of the family*, he thought.

He fished his pillow off the floor, stuck it behind his head, and muscled his eyes closed. He forced himself to take slow, even breaths. In the unguarded borderland between awake and asleep, a memory of his mom slipped in. His whole class had been invited to a birthday party, which was probably the only reason *he* had been. This was toward the end, when he was absent from school as often as he was present. And sure enough, he was too sick to go. His mom brought home ice cream and sat next to him as he curled up on the couch. He managed only one bite, but she finished the bowl and pretended they'd "shared" it. "Thanks for the ice cream," he'd said. "It was good." She'd reached over and smoothed out his hair, the worry lines around her eyes bunching up as she smiled.

But sleep came and took her away from him again. In her place, a nightmare. Alex was back in the Stung Man's underground tomb, carved out of an abandoned subway station and furnished with stolen luxuries. A large black scorpion scrabbled over the fringe of a rug, and then a shadow fell over it. Alex looked up and there he was: the Stung Man, his face bloated with ancient stings and his robes smelling faintly of decay. He raised his left arm, which ended not in a hand but a massive scorpion stinger. The barbed point was the size of a carving knife. The stinger flashed forward —

Alex woke with a start. He sat up so fast that he nearly hit his forehead on the little TV screen in the seat in front of him. *So much for getting some shut-eye*, he thought. He looked around. The problem was the plane, this long, dark cabin. It was too much like one of the stone sarcophagi back at the Metropolitan Museum of Art, where his mom had worked as a curator before she disappeared.

He looked at the little screen, feeling both tired and restless. TV would be a good distraction.

He glanced around to make sure no one was looking. The businessman in the aisle seat was fast asleep, chin on shirt, drool on chin. Alex reached into his collar and fished his amulet out from under his blue polo shirt. It was made of polished stone and refined copper and shaped like a sacred scarab beetle, a symbol of regeneration in ancient Egypt. It had been his mom's, and now, it seemed, it was his.

Alex was still learning what the ancient artifact could do. He knew one thing, though. Considering it had been made in a time and place where towering stone pyramids were the height of technology, the amulet made a surprisingly good remote. He closed his hand around the stone scarab and felt the rush he did whenever he used the amulet. His pulse revved and his mind focused; he felt like a race car driver rounding a curve.

The little screen blinked to life and he selected MOVIES, not with his fingers but with his eyes, and began flipping through his choices.

"What're you watchin'?"

Alex gasped.

"Must be a scary movie," said Ren, poking him in the shoulder.

"You just, kind of — you shouldn't surprise people like that," said Alex, keeping his voice low so he wouldn't wake the beefy businessman.

"You shouldn't zone out playing with your toy," said Ren.

Alex looked down at the scarab. He knew she was just joking. It wasn't a toy: It had already saved both their lives. He slipped it back under his collar.

Ren reached up and touched the screen in front of her. The first thing that came up was the flight map. Alex saw her scan the screen and read the numbers along the side. It was a British airline, and the distances were all in kilometers.

He watched her eyes narrow, her brow crease. She got one very distinct line right between her eyebrows when she concentrated. Alex thought of it as the ON button of a brown-eyed computer.

"You're converting kilometers to miles, aren't you?" he said.

"Yep," she said. "It's easy."

"Oh yeah?" he said. He knew her too well to believe her.

Ren wasn't the type of brainiac for whom things came easy; Ren was the type who worked problems to death. "What's 2,389 kilometers?" he said, reading the screen.

Again, the crease. "About 1,500 miles," she said. "Maybe a little less."

Alex didn't doubt her math. Her dad was one of the chief engineers at the Metropolitan Museum, and the apple hadn't fallen far from the tree. It's just that it was a very small apple — almost a crab apple, really. She was twelve, like him, but not quite four and a half feet tall. From her seat, she had to look not only over at Alex, but also up.

There was a rumbling next to them. The businessman was climbing to his feet, looking back over his shoulder to see if there was a line for the restrooms. Alex turned back to Ren. "Wanna watch a movie?"

But Ren's eyes were on the businessman. "Let's go over the plan while he's away," she said as soon as he headed down the aisle.

Alex rolled his eyes.

"What?" said Ren.

"Never mind," said Alex, but then he said it anyway. "What good will going over the plan up here do? We need to get down on the ground and start looking."

"We need to know what we're doing before we do it!" she countered.

Alex almost rolled his eyes again. It was such a Ren thing to say. A phrase the other kids used to say popped into his mind: Plus Ten Ren. Ren the planner, Ren the extra-credit gobbler . . .

"So, no movie?" he said.

She shook her head again. "This is *important*, Alex."

He took one last look at the screen and let out an exaggerated sigh. They'd been over all this before they left, but he knew she wouldn't yield. "Fine," he said.

Ren heard the sigh but ignored it. She knew Alex wasn't much of a planner. She even sort of understood it: For most of his life, his unpredictable health had made planning a waste of time. But he was better now, and this was serious. The Lost Spells his mom had used to bring him back from the brink of death had brought others back, too: Death Walkers. And the next one, they believed, was in London.

When she thought about it, she got the same flash of fear she got before tests. A pit-of-the-stomach panic she could almost taste. It used to be: *Was she ready? Had she prepared enough to keep up with her classmates? What kind of grade would she bring home to her brilliant parents?* She swallowed hard, knowing how much higher the stakes were now. The new questions: *Was she ready? Had she prepared enough to face the new dangers ahead of them? Would she make it home at all?*

"Okay," she said, leaning in and lowering her voice. She began with what she already knew. That always settled her down some. "The Stung Man came from the museum. Which makes sense, because where else are you going to find a mummified ancient Egyptian? And we needed your scarab amulet and the spell — the *right* spell — from the Book of the Dead to send him back. That came from the museum, too."

She paused to see if Alex wanted to add anything, but all he said was, "Obviously."

She shot him a look. His expression was flat, and he was drumming his fingers on his thigh in a way that was starting to annoy her. *What part of an evil spirit clinging to the edge of the afterlife and escaping at the first opportunity is obvious?* she thought. *Since when?*

She went on. "And things started to happen all over the world as soon as the Spells were used. So things have been happening in London for a while now."

Alex perked up, finally met Ren's eyes. "This one's been awake longer," he said.

"Yeah," she said. "So?"

But he was thinking about it now, and all he did was repeat that one word: "Longer . . ."

He hadn't even been paying attention, but he'd figured something out. Something important. Ren hated it when people did that to her. *WHAT?* she wanted to say, but she didn't want to look stupid. She hated that even more. "Anyway," she said, "the main thing is the Death Walker."

Alex looked at her, bug-eyed. "The main thing is my mom!"

"Right," said Ren. "But we don't even know if she's in London."

"She's there," said Alex.

"Okay, but let's just —"

"Right, right, right," said Alex, not bothering to hide his impatience. "We know The Order is working with the Death Walkers. And we know The Order has my mom, so if we find them, we'll find her."

Ren didn't argue. They were pretty sure the ancient death cult had kidnapped Alex's mom when they'd stolen the Lost Spells. But *pretty sure* wasn't the same as *knowing* — and she really wished he'd stop drumming his fingers like that.

"Anyway," she said, glancing down at the offending digits. "The first thing we need to find out is who — or what, I guess — this Death Walker is —"

"We need to get down there and get started," said Alex, cutting her off.

She opened her mouth to respond, but he cut her off again. "All right?" he said. "Period."

"All right," she said, sitting back in her seat. "But stop doing that thing with your fingers. It's annoying."

Both their seats were jolted as the bulky businessman thumped back down. If the conversation wasn't over before, it was now.

Alex went back to picking his movie, and Ren stared silently out her window at the red light of dawn. She'd go over it all one more time, on her own.

Crash Landing

Before Alex's movie even ended in Row 22, another drama began to unfold in the cockpit. "I don't like the look of those clouds," said the copilot.

The captain glanced over and then did a quick double take, his eyes zeroing in on the radar screen. "Those weren't there a minute ago," said Captain Martin Hadley. He was one of the airline's most experienced pilots, but as he watched the new clouds spinning slowly in the opposite direction of the ones around them, he got the sinking feeling he was about to experience something entirely new.

The copilot swallowed hard. He was nervous for the opposite reason: very little experience. They were both watching the small screen closely when air traffic control came on over the cockpit radio. They were watching the same thing in the tower.

"What *is* that?" said Captain Hadley.

For a few long moments, there was no reply, then: "Be advised, Flight 768 . . ." The voice started strong and official but then seemed to break under its own weight: "We have no idea what that is . . . but you're heading directly into it."

The copilot reached up and loosened the collar of his crisp white shirt. The captain crossed himself. "Reroute?" he said into the handset. He took a look at the fuel gauge, did some quick calculations: How long could they circle? What other airports could they make it to?

Another pause on the other end and then: "Negative. It's small, low speed. Let's just get you down."

"Roger that," said the captain.

"It *is* small, isn't it?" said the copilot, seeking reassurance.

"I suppose," said Hadley, peering into the rosy morning light ahead of them. "But what is it?"

An hour later, descending through light rain into their final approach, they found out.

Thick drops of something red hit the cockpit windows, staining them pink as it mixed with the wind and water. The engines began to choke on the stuff, and the big plane bucked like a spooked horse. The captain wrestled with the U-shaped yoke, his knuckles turning white as the windows began to turn red.

"Pull up! Pull up!" shouted the copilot, but Hadley ignored him. There'd be no pulling up now: too late for that. They were landing, one way or the other.

"As a precaution due to extreme conditions, we have to ask you to prepare for a potential crash landing." The announcement sounded through the cabin and cut into people's headphones. A thunderous noise filled the air as questions were shouted and a hundred urgent conversations began. The announcement continued, momentarily drowning it all out: "Please make sure your seat belts are fastened securely and your window shades are closed."

Ren had, quite possibly, been the only one paying attention when the flight crew went over emergency procedures pre-flight. Even so, it was hard to remember all the details with her pulse suddenly pounding wildly in her ears. She reached over and flicked down the plastic shade, catching one more glimpse of the rosy morning light.

She looked at Alex. "This is bad," she shouted over the frantic voices filling the cabin.

Alex looked over and agreed wordlessly, his wide-open eyes and slowly bobbing head doing the talking.

The plane bucked again, sending a flight attendant who'd been trying to demonstrate the crash-landing position into a crash landing on her backside. Half a dozen passengers screamed as if they'd just witnessed a murder.

Others had already assumed the position, determined to ride this thing out, for better or worse, with their heads between their knees. The burly businessman next to them was sitting bolt upright and releasing odd, high-pitched yelps as he began to hyperventilate.

"Should we, you know?" shouted Alex. His voice cracked on the last part, giving away his fear. He mimed assuming the crash-landing position, raising both fists up toward his ears and ducking his head down between them.

Ren felt a sudden, desperate need to know how close they were to the ground. She cracked open the shade, noticing, as if from a distance, that her hands were shaking. In the two-inch gap, she saw a line of red briefly streak across the pink background.

"Oh, please no," she murmured. The small sound was swallowed up by the hysteria all around her, but Alex had seen her reaction. He followed her eyes to the window as she reached over and flicked up the shade.

They both saw it now. The morning light was too rosy — and too dark. Two more long tendrils of red snaked across the surface of the window.

They'd heard about this: red rain in London. Some people said it was blood; others said it couldn't possibly be. It had always turned back to regular rain in the end — and the few samples people had managed to collect had turned right back with it.

Magic, Ren knew, was always hard to pin down.

BOOOOM!

A sound like artillery roared from the massive jet engine on the opposite wing. Whatever was falling out there, the plane didn't like it one bit. The engines on both wings began to groan and shake. A sound like a dying giant filled the cabin.

"We can't land in this stuff!" shouted Alex.

Ren looked down. Through the red haze, she could see the ground now. Rooftops whizzed by below, like a city of dollhouses. The houses ended. The airport was just up ahead, the slick, red runway . . .

"We're about to!" she called back.

One final announcement rang out, shouted and ampli-fied but barely audible over the commotion: "Crash-landing positions!"

Ren's head was swirling with panic and confusion as she buried it in her lap.

What was falling out there?

Would it turn back to regular rain?

The plane was shaking so violently it seemed on the verge of flying apart.

Would it be too late when it did?

She laced her fingers behind her head, pictured her par-ents, and braced for impact.

The wheels were down and the time was up. Captain Hadley surveyed the scene ahead of him. The wind whipped the red rain across the cockpit windows as he stared at the runway with wide-open, unblinking eyes. The white lines had turned pink and the lights glowed red, but he thought he could see them well enough.

"What am I looking at?" he yelled into the radio. It wasn't an idle question. If it was just red rain, that was one thing. He'd landed in rain more times than he could count. But if it was what it looked like . . .

"Unclassified meteorological phenomenon," came the reply.

The copilot spat out a reply of his own: "Unclassified, my —"

"Not now!" barked Hadley, cutting him off. "Eyes on the instruments!"

The plane touched down with a heavy bang. A sick hiss rose as the wheels met the tarmac and the red liquid. That much speed and power and weight would vaporize water, the captain knew, effectively taking it out of the equation. But this seemed to be a stickier, trickier substance.

The wheels burned and hissed along the runway, and the plane began to turn. Captain Hadley got a sick, empty feeling in his gut as the big airliner went into a skid.

He took one last look over at his copilot. The man was folded over in crash-landing position and screaming into his own knees. So Hadley was on his own, then: on his own and in charge of the lives of hundreds. He let out a long, slow breath.

He had the wings on his collar, and he had the responsibility.

Instead of a death grip on the control yoke, he forced himself to take a light one as the plane veered to the side. *Muscle it and you'll end up upside down*, he told himself. Instead of squinting his eyes half shut, he opened them. *Look. Watch.*

He made himself breathe. He made himself think.

Don't think of it as water; think of it as mud.

The massive plane corrected, the nose began to straighten out slightly. Still too much of an angle, still heading toward the edge of the runway, but with every foot that passed, the massive plane slowed just a little more.

The captain stayed calm. He remembered his training and, against all odds, he brought the big bird home to its nest. The plane came to a halt, slightly sideways and a stone's throw from the edge of the runway.

Safe.

Welcome to London

Alex and Ren stumbled up the Jetway on wobbly knees. As soon as they arrived in the terminal, they saw Luke up ahead amid the scrum of passengers and airline personnel. Alex looked out the big glass windows at the rain coming down. Just regular rain now. It had turned over during the plane's slow taxi to the gate. Outside, the last pinkish reminders of their ordeal were washing away.

His head was buzzing and his nerves were shot. He jumped slightly as the loudspeaker came on above him. A crisp female voice: "Flight 768 from New York, now arriving." The shaken passengers stopped to listen. Perhaps there'd be some explanation? "Welcome to London!" the voice concluded brightly.

Alex turned to Ren and they just shook their heads. Even after weeks of widespread weirdness, the world of the living was still firmly in the denial stage. Ren looked away first, and Alex wondered if part of her was still in that stage, too.

They caught up with Luke, but a man in an airline uniform was already talking to him. "And of course we are particularly concerned that our first-class passengers not be alarmed by this fluke occurrence," the man purred in a posh British accent.

"It's cool, bro," said Luke. "I slept through most of it anyway."

The man smiled politely, slightly baffled. "You . . . slept . . ."

"What was that stuff?" asked Ren, busting in.

The man looked over, straightening his red blazer.

"It was blood, wasn't it?" said Alex.

The man looked over at Luke as if to say: *You know these two?*

Luke shrugged. "He's my cousin. They were in coach."

The man gave a quick nod. *That explains it.* "We think it was algae," he said without much conviction.

"Algae?" said Alex. "Seriously?"

"Yes," sniffed the man, "an aerial bloom of red algae. It's quite common at sea."

"It's quite common *in* the sea," corrected Ren.

The man looked down at her but quickly looked away, as shifty as a dog caught pulling food off the counter. A large Australian standing nearby broke in: "That was no bloomin' algae!"

"Come on, let's go," said Alex. He knew they weren't going to get any real information out of this tall red mouthpiece.

Ren nodded and Luke loped along with them as they left the two men to argue over aerial bloom versus aerial blood.

Alex looked over at his cousin. Luke was a year and a half

older, half a foot taller, and infinitely more muscled. "Did you really sleep through all that?"

"Most of it." Luke shrugged. "Killer workout yesterday. Totally wiped. Sorry I missed the algae, though."

Alex's jaw dropped open. "Do you seriously think that was red algae?"

"That's what the man said," said Luke.

Alex looked over at Ren, expecting her to mirror his disappointment.

"Well," she said. "I heard that sometimes, like, frogs and things get sucked up in funnel clouds and then fall back to earth. Maybe . . ."

Alex just shook his head. He expected the airline to be in denial, not his friends. They headed for the passport control room. A big sign near the entrance read: UK BORDER.

"It's cool that you can have a border in a building," said Luke. "But I guess you can have a building on a border so . . ."

He trailed off and a quick smile flickered across Alex's face. Family spy or not, he sometimes got a kick out of his cousin.

"Look at the lines," said Ren.

Alex sized them up. "Not too bad."

"Exactly," said Ren, flapping a London guidebook toward him. "The book says they're usually huge: 'Pack one snack for the international flight, and another for the passport control lines.'"

"That's because we're the only ones daft enough to come here now," said a voice behind them.

The three friends turned around and saw an older couple. The man who'd spoken was wearing a sweater vest and a friendly smile. "No offense," he added.

"Because of the algae?" said Luke.

The man and woman both gave him patient looks, trying not to look pitying. "Not just that," said the man. "Graves been robbed, people gone missing . . ."

"Yeah, we heard about some of that," Alex began, pointing between Ren and himself with one thumb and leaving Luke out of it.

He was going to say more, but the man's face clouded over and the smile fell away. "Our little . . ." he began. "Our little nephew, Robbie . . ."

The woman patted her husband on the back and took over. "Our nephew up and vanished. Lives with my sister on Swain's Lane. We don't think he's . . . like the others . . . He's an energetic boy, you know, probably just off on some adventure."

Now Alex was the one trying not to look pitying. Before his mom had used the spells, he'd spent most of his life deathly ill. He knew better than almost anyone what it was like to put on a brave face, to pretend things were better than they were.

"So you're here to help?"

"Help look for him!" said the man, stuffing some cheer back into his voice. "Get out there and beat the bushes!"

Alex hadn't heard the phrase before, but he liked it. That's what he was there for, too.

"Where are your parents, by the way?" said the woman, scanning what was left of the line in front of them. She had her hair up in a bun, wore a floral dress, and looked like everyone's aunt ever.

Luke began to say something, but Ren cut him off. "I'm supposed to call them!"

"Oh, that's good," said the woman. "They'll pick you up?"

Alex and Ren just smiled. The woman took a quick look at the group: three different shades of hair, three different tones of skin. Alex was half-Egyptian with shaggy black hair and tan skin; Luke looked like a mini Viking; and Ren fell somewhere in between, brown-haired, brown-eyed, and pint-sized.

"Well," said the lady, pulling something from her handbag. "If you happen to see our Robbie, at a playground or a McDonald's or the like . . ."

Even before she unfolded the paper, Alex knew it would be a Missing Person flyer. His heart sank when he saw it. In the color photo in the center, the boy's face was flushed and smiling, and he was holding up a third-place trophy with a soccer ball on top. Alex noticed the blue eyes and light brown hair first. Then he noticed that one of the boy's eyebrows was a little higher than the other, giving his face a slightly off-kilter look. He looked like the kind of healthy, normal kid Alex had always wanted to be.

He looked up at the woman, sure of two things: that he would recognize this boy if he saw him, and that he never would see him. Not alive anyway. She pressed the paper toward him, and he couldn't help but take a step back.

Ren stepped forward and took it. "We'll keep an eye out!" she said. She shot Alex a look as she turned to put the paper in her carry-on bag.

Alex looked down at the tile floor, trying to pull it together. Death, magic, evil . . . All the things they thought they'd put to rest in New York were here waiting for them in London. The missing boy gave a face to a familiar thought: *Is this all my fault, just like New York? Does me being here help — or make things worse?*

He turned to Ren, but she was busy getting her passport and customs form ready. They were at the front of the line.

He handed the border control agent his passport. The man leaned forward in his chair and looked behind Alex. "You here by yourself, then?" he said, sitting back and eye-balling the passport.

"With her," said Alex, pointing to Ren in the next line.

The man frowned. "Purpose of visit?"

Alex rattled off the answer he'd prepared: that Dr. Ernst Todtman at the Met had sent them to intern with Dr. Priya Aditi at the British Museum.

"What kind of doctors?" said the official.

"Egyptologists," said Alex.

The man looked at him carefully, paused, then broke into a broad smile. "Who on earth would make up a story like that?" he said, handing him his passport. "Welcome to the United Kingdom."

The last one through, Alex joined the other two.

"We just crossed the border," said Luke, still amused by the concept.

"You're an international athlete now," said Alex.

"Oh yeah!" said Luke, puffing out his broad chest a bit more as the three walked straight into an airport in crisis.

The long lines they'd expected entering the country were on the other side, desperately trying to leave London. Security lines snaked back and forth, threatening to stretch out the sliding doors. Electronic boards flashed delays and cancellations after the mysterious squall. Raised voices and wailing infants echoed off the terminal's high ceilings.

Ren took a modest clump of British bills from her pocket and stopped by an airport kiosk. Alex surveyed the unfamiliar candy choices — Aero, Wispa, Double Decker — as Ren bought a newspaper that had caught her eye.

She handed it over and Alex read the huge front-page headline for himself: "ROYAL ROBBERY: Crown Jewels Stolen!" Below that, in type only slightly smaller: "A Dozen Priceless Pieces Taken from Tower of London." Next to it, there was a picture of a massive, jewel-encrusted crown.

The familiar phrases popped out at Alex as he skimmed the story: "time locks disabled . . . alarms failed to sound . . . cameras turned toward the wall." It was just like the day the Lost Spells had been stolen from the Met. The day the Spells had been stolen and his mom had disappeared.

He flipped to the next page, and the picture stopped him cold. It was a hand, in extreme close-up, reaching up to disable one last camera. The hand was wrapped tightly in linen. He understood immediately that it was a mummy. But he'd never seen ancient linen look so clean before . . .

He held the paper open for Ren to see. She nodded. *Was she thinking the same thing he was?* He wanted to ask but . . .

"Got to *hand* it to that guy, huh?" said Luke, leaning in for a look of his own. "Won't be getting any fingerprints off him!"

They ignored his joke and exchanged questions with their eyes. Luke noticed. "If I didn't know better, I'd think you two didn't always want me around," he said.

"That's crazy," said Alex as Ren took the paper and stuffed it into her carry-on bag.

"Well, don't sweat it, cuz," said Luke. "I'll be out of your hair in no time." He pointed up at a sign that read UNDER-GROUND, with a stylized train logo next to it. "Taking the train to the training."

They swung by baggage claim on the way out. Ren wrestled her perfectly packed wheelie bag off the carousel, Alex fished a heavy leather suitcase off the belt and grunted as he thunked it to the floor, and Luke plucked a large duffel bag free as if he were lifting a candy bar. Not that he ate candy bars.

Then the three wheeled, walked, and lugged their way out of the airport. For a while the signs for the trains and ground transport were right next to each other, but eventually the arrows pointed in opposite directions.

"Where are you two staying, again?" said Luke, holding up his phone, ready to punch in the info. "I'm supposed to ch — I mean, it would be cool to hang out."

Alex and Ren exchanged quick glances.

"Umm, well," said Alex.

"Umwell?" said Luke. "Is that, like, a hotel?"

Alex couldn't tell if he was joking.

"Alex Sennefer?" came a gruff voice. "Renata Duran?"

The friends turned around and saw a very large man with a surprisingly small flat cap pulled down tightly on his large shaved head.

"Uh, yeah?" said Alex. "That's us."

"Thought it looked like you," said the man, holding up a piece of paper and looking from it to Alex and Ren. "'At's you, all right."

Alex was having a hard time understanding.

"'Pologize fer me accent," said the man. "Must sound a bit like I've got marbles in me mouf."

Alex searched his brain: *What's a mouf?*

"Fing is, Dr. Aditi couldn't make it, see? Sent me to pick you up an' all 'at, right?"

Alex watched the man closely. He could understand a dozen different ancient Egyptian dialects with the help of his amulet. He hadn't missed one word of the Stung Man's Middle Kingdom bluster. But this giant gent had him baffled.

Ren stepped up: "'E says — excuse me, *he* says that Dr. Aditi can't make it."

The man nodded. "In a meeting, she is."

"She's in a meeting, and she sent him to pick us up."

"Bring you to the museum."

"And bring us —"

"I got that part," said Alex. He sized the man up. Size: XXL. He knew who they were, and he knew Dr. Aditi was supposed to meet them — but who *was* he?

"Are you, like, her assistant?" asked Ren skeptically.

"Aw, nuffin' like 'at," said the man, who definitely didn't seem the scholarly type. "I'm a driver. Fer the museum, like."

Alex nodded. That made more sense.

"Look at you two, with your own driver," said Luke. "I'm just gonna head to the train."

"Who's this, then?" said the man — *Ooze iss den?* — looking down at his sheet of paper again.

"Luke Bauer, big guy, remember the name." He turned to Alex and added, "Got your digits, cuz. I'll send you a text — or look you up at the Umwell."

He slung his duffel bag over his shoulder and headed off toward the airport train station.

"'Is way, den," said the man. "Got a van out front."

"Come on," Ren said to Alex. "Let's get out of here."

"I can 'elp you wiv 'at bag, any'ow," offered the man, stepping forward and plucking Alex's heavy suitcase from the ground with one massive bear paw.

Alex nodded. He wasn't about to argue with that. He decided he was probably just being paranoid. Ren seemed to trust the guy. She was a few steps ahead, chatting away with him. She understood him just fine. Had she studied that in preparation for the trip, too? He picked up the pace and caught up with them.

"What's your name, anyway?" he said to the man.

"Me name?"

"Yeah, you name."

"It's Liam, innit?" he said.

Alex was confused again. *Is he asking me?*

Ren read his expression. "It's Liam, Alex."

"Okay, cool. Nice to meet you."

The man reached up and touched the tip of his undersized cap with his free hand. "Just up a'ead 'ere," he said, pointing to a pair of large sliding doors.

Alex nodded. He was beginning to understand the man's accent. Rule #1: No *h*'s. The automatic doors shooshed open, and Alex took one last look at the chaotic airport as they left it behind. They'd flown thousands of miles: out of trouble and chaos and danger in one city and into a fresh batch of it in another. It would be worth it if his mom was here. She had to be, and once he found her, she'd know what to do. She always had . . .

On the other side of the doors was a dim lower level, two narrow lanes of pavement with a curb on one side and a low concrete wall on the other. There was a beat-up cargo van directly in front of them — the kind with a sliding door and no windows in the back — and that was it.

"Where are all the cars?" said Alex. "The airport's so busy inside . . ."

"Bit of a dustup," said Liam, pointing vaguely to the top of the ramp. "I was d'last one got frew."

Alex looked up to the top of the ramp. There was a car sideways across both lanes. A man standing nearby had both arms in the air and another man was shouting something at him. Alex looked the other way. Another ramp led up and away, merging with the traffic leaving the airport. "Did they crash or —"

But before he could finish his question, his own heavy suitcase crashed into him. Liam swung the thing like a Ping-Pong paddle, clocking Alex hard on the shoulder and sending him sprawling to the pavement.

"Kuhhh!" he said as the air escaped his lungs. The pavement dug into his palms as he landed. Out of the corner of his eye, he saw Liam bring the suitcase down toward Ren, trying to swat her like a fly. She leapt nimbly to the side, but the heavy case just clipped her leg and sent her to the ground, too.

This guy is *a fake!* he thought. He began to scramble to his feet, but the suitcase came down on his head, knocking him senseless.

Through half-closed eyes he saw Ren rushing back toward the airport — and then knocked flat by the swinging suitcase. *No!*

Liam dropped the suitcase and crouched down over Alex. He fastened one plastic zip tie around his wrists and another around his hands, tying them together in prayer position. Alex pulled against them helplessly. He rolled onto his back and brought the first plastic band up to his teeth: useless, like trying to bite through a Coke bottle.

He had one last hope. Alex tried to grasp his amulet, but with his hands bound together he could only press his thumbs to the thing. Not enough: The scarab remained cold and inert. *This man knew exactly what to do*, thought Alex, *and that means one thing: The Order.*

He flopped onto his side and looked across the pavement toward Ren. His friend was splayed out ten feet away. Her hands weren't tied, but she wasn't moving. A fresh wave of panic rolled through him, and then he heard the van's side door slide open.

Alex tried to stand. Even with his head still ringing from the blow, he knew that if this man got them in that van, they would never be seen again.

All Alex managed to do was sit up.

"There y'are, ya little biter," said Liam, looking down at him. "I 'ope y'understand me now."

As he reached down for Alex, a shoulder slammed hard into Liam's gut and a pair of arms wrapped up the tops of his thick legs. It was a textbook tackle, with the blond head off to one side of Liam's hip. Luke.

Flawless technique allowed him to take the much larger man down. Liam's mouth formed a perfect round O as he fell backward and his head slammed into the side of the van. The two bodies went down in a heap, but Luke was up a half-second later, springing to his feet like a jungle cat.

"My hands!" Alex called, holding the plastic-tied appendages up for his cousin.

"Right," said Luke. He took one more look over at Liam, still motionless on the ground, and then rushed over to try to loosen the ties.

"You came back," said Alex, stating the obvious. He knew he still wasn't thinking as clearly as he needed to.

Luke gave him a sly smile. "Didn't trust that guy for a second."

The ties wouldn't budge. Once fastened, they had to be cut free. Both boys looked over at Ren. She'd trusted this big ham hock of a man — and paid the price.

The good news: She was starting to sit up now.

The bad news: So was the ham hock!

Hot Pursuit

"Ren!" yelled Alex.

She stood up on wobbly Bambi legs.

Alex looked over his shoulder as he and Luke yanked her forward. The oversized thug had pushed himself up to one knee, and the slap of boots on pavement alerted Alex to three more men racing down the ramp. The grim looks on their faces told him they weren't coming to help.

The three kids took off running, but it took Alex and Ren a few steps to get up to speed. Luke could've left them in the dust but hung back to help as they headed up the opposite side of the ramp, away from the disabled car and toward the exit. Alex panicked when he saw the upslope. Hills had always been a major challenge for him. Then he remembered: *That was before.* His legs found their rhythm and began driving him smoothly up the ramp.

There were four men in pursuit now. The other three looked lean and hungry, like a pack of wolves, and were

34

already overtaking their beefy buddy, who had wobbled to his feet.

Alex pawed uselessly at his amulet with his bound hands.

"We need to reach the top of the ramp!" called Ren.

Her short legs pumped hard on the upslope, and her sneakers slapped the pavement, but she wasn't moving fast enough. Alex held back, unwilling to leave her behind. And with each step, the wolves pulled closer. They were ten yards behind . . . eight . . . six . . .

MEEEEEEP! MEEEEEEP!

A tiny car careened into view like a tin-plated, turbo-charged golf cart. It fishtailed around the corner at the top of the ramp before barreling down the slope.

"Watch out!" called Alex. All three friends dove to the side to avoid the speeding vehicle.

The little machine whizzed past them in a red-and-white blur, heading straight for the wolf pack. The four men scattered like bowling pins, half diving to the left and half to the right. As they hit the pavement, the undersized engine shifted into reverse. The sound was less mighty roar than feverish whine, but the tiny car zoomed backward up the ramp and slammed to a stop in front of the fallen friends. A tall lady with striking features leaned out the open driver's-side window. "Get in!" she shouted.

Painted on the door below her in red letters:

THE BRITISH MUSEUM

"Dr. Aditi?" shouted Ren.

"Sorry I'm late!" the woman called.

The three friends ran around to the passenger side and piled clown car–style into the little vehicle. With no time to push the seatback forward, Ren vaulted between the seats. Alex attempted to do the same but got caught up. A solid shove from Luke finished the job. The taller cousin plopped down in the front passenger seat and the little car was moving again before he even slammed the door.

Fists pounded on the hood and side of the car. Alex was afraid the thugs would capsize the so-called automobile with their size and muscle. Liam's large fleshy face appeared at the window nearest Alex, who was still trying to untangle himself from his friend in the tiny backseat.

"Where's your luggage?" Dr. Aditi shouted over the combined racket of men and machine.

"My what?" said Alex. He'd forgotten all about his suitcase — except for the part where it had come down on his head.

"At the bottom of the ramp!" shouted Ren.

"Right, then," said Aditi. She brought her chin down in a sharp nod and her foot down in a sharp stomp. The car came to an abrupt stop. Four thick thumps rocked it as the pursuers bounced into and off of its angled frame.

Aditi floored it. A quick bump inside the car coincided

with a sharp yelp outside. *Was that someone's foot?* wondered Alex. He hoped so.

And just like that, the little car was racing back the way they'd come. Aditi screeched to another halt near the van. "Would you mind terribly?" she said to Luke.

He jumped out of the passenger side and tossed Alex's battered briefcase into the open door. Alex was useless with his hands tied, so Ren wrestled the thing into the backseat. Out the back window, the thugs were gaining again — except for the one with the fresh limp.

"Hurry!" called Alex. It seemed like a lot of fuss for luggage and he considered saying so, but he knew that no one liked a backseat driver.

Luke tossed in Ren's wheelie bag then jumped back in, holding his own duffel. A fist smacked the back window as the car hightailed it the wrong way up the ramp, toward the disabled car. Aditi revved the engine and bumped the little car up on the curb to get around the sideways sedan. She bounced and jostled over another curb to get into the next lane.

And just like that, they were on their way out of the airport. Aditi downshifted, and everyone — the little car included — seemed to take a long, deep breath.

Aditi adjusted her mirror and looked around. "So," she said brightly, "how was the flight?"

At a small executive airport outside the city, another, smoother flight had just touched down. The pilot of this one had not been at all surprised by the red rain and, with plenty of fuel, had simply circled above the clouds, waiting for it to end. The sleek private jet taxied to a halt, and a lone passenger disembarked. He was tall and gaunt with spiky silver hair, and he carried a long black case in one hand.

No one asked this man how his flight was as he walked into the small main building. No one said anything to him at all, just tried to avoid his eyes.

No chance of that. Perched atop a long, sharp nose, his eyes were dark and cold and predatory. They took in the room at a glance and identified the approaching threat immediately. Even at small airports, there are rules. Even at small airports, there are international borders.

A young, blue-shirted customs official named Lewis broke the silence. "Sorry I'm late, Dave," he said as he rushed into the room to relieve his coworker. "My car wouldn't start."

Dave wheeled around and stared at him in surprise. Lewis wasn't late; he was early.

Dave had debts and needed the money. In a word, he'd been bribed. And part of his job had been to disable Lewis's car. He simply hadn't disabled it enough. Now he tried to warn his coworker off with a sharp look and a shake of his head, but Lewis had no idea what any of that meant. He ignored it and got to work.

38

"Right," he said, turning to the silver-haired man who had approached the desk. "Let's see your passport."

The room fell completely silent. Everyone there — Dave, the pilot, a safety inspector, even a few members of the ground crew — they all knew the deal. Everyone except Lewis.

"I'm afraid I don't have one," said the man slowly.

"You . . . I'm sorry . . . What?" said Lewis. "Listen, mate, this is a small airport, things are a little looser maybe, but you still need the basics."

He turned toward Dave with a *Can you believe this guy?* smile. But Dave was not smiling. In fact, he was trembling slightly.

He mouthed three words, slowly and distinctly, and underlined their importance with his eyes: "Let. It. Go."

Lewis looked at him closely. He was just now hearing the silence, sensing the fear, and beginning to put things together. He didn't know what was going on, but he knew it wasn't legal. "Aw, Dave," he said, the disappointment clear in his voice. "You know I can't do that."

He turned back to face the man, but the man's face was no longer there. In its place was a long iron mask in the shape of a crocodile head. The black bag lay empty on the floor.

Lewis flinched, more from surprise than fear, at first. From flat scales to blunt teeth, the detail in the dull gray iron was impressive. The man stared out coldly through eyeholes above the snout. And then he raised his hand, and an ancient power flowed forth. That's when the fear started. The fear, and the pain.

Switcharoo

Alex squirmed in the microscopic backseat of Aditi's car. There was no place to put the heavy suitcase, so he hugged it under his bound hands and watched as Dr. Aditi darted through traffic.

"Uh, lady? You're on the wrong side of the road!" yelped Luke.

Aditi looked over at him, smiled, downshifted, and stomped on the gas. "Not over here, luv," she said.

Ren ducked her head between the seats. "They drive on the left in England," she shouted over the sound of the overworked engine.

Aditi executed a daring double pass, darting between two larger cars, both of which honked angrily.

Alex followed her eyes. She was spending at least as much time looking in the rearview mirror as she was watching where she was going. He wouldn't have minded if they weren't going quite so fast, or if their vehicle offered more than a soup-can level of protection. He hugged his suitcase tighter.

"I can keep an eye out for the van if you want to watch the road!" he called.

"You think they'll follow us?" said Ren, wheeling around to look out the back window.

"Not necessarily . . ." Aditi began.

Alex saw Ren's shoulders relax a little.

"They might be waiting for us when we get there," Aditi added.

Ren's shoulders bunched up again. Alex remembered the museum's name, painted in red on the car door. *What was Aditi thinking? She'd given away their destination!*

"I think you're right," said Luke during a brief lull in the traffic noise.

"About what?" said Aditi, scanning a side mirror.

"Everyone else is driving on the left, too," he said. "Just, you know, slower."

Now Aditi looked over at him. "I'm sorry," she said. "Who are you?"

"I'm Luke," he said.

Aditi looked at him blankly.

"I'm his cousin," he said, hooking a thumb back toward Alex.

"But Todtman didn't mention . . ." Aditi continued. Her eyes found Alex's in the mirror again, and she gave him a *What's the deal?* look.

"He's not, like, with us," said Alex. "He's here for sports camp."

He leaned forward as far as his bulky suitcase would allow. "Luke, man, you can't say anything about this to your mom and dad, all right?"

"What, why not?" he protested. "It's a good story!"

"Come on, man!" pleaded Alex. His aunt and uncle were his legal guardians with his mom missing, and he was afraid they'd have him on the next plane home.

"I'm just kidding, man," said Luke. "This camp is gonna rock, but if the 'rents found out they're snatching up American kids over here, they'd have me home before my first high jump."

Alex leaned back and exhaled, glad they were more or less on the same page.

"But they'll probably hear about the algae thing on the news," added Luke.

London's towering center loomed up in front of them as they quickly left the city's outskirts behind. They melted the zip ties off with the car's lighter as they bumblebeed down the highway. At every point along the way, at least one of them was looking back, either in the mirrors or out the rear window.

Finally, they reached their exit. Alex scanned the signs as they made the turn: BLOOMSBURY, FITZROVIA, BRITISH MUSEUM . . .

Alex tried to make eye contact again in the mirror, but Aditi was too busy merging back into the city traffic. The Order had already known who was meeting them at the airport — he could still hear Liam mangling Aditi's name — and they would definitely know where they were headed now. He hoped she knew what she was doing. He watched her eyes work as she drove, quick and alert. He knew she was a member of the same secret group of scholars as Todtman. Ren called them "the book club," and there was no doubt they were a far-flung group of museum-working nerds — but they were also mysterious and powerful. Alex wondered if Aditi had an amulet, too, something to match Todtman's formidable falcon.

He looked back through the window. *No van*, he thought. *Not yet.* And as the light changed and they scooted through a busy intersection, he thought he might be able to keep it that way. His head was clearer now, and his hands were free. He reached up and wrapped his left hand around his scarab amulet. The rush overtook him, and he looked back again, feeling his pulse quicken as he narrowed his eyes.

He stared at the traffic light and it instantly turned red. A chorus of honks rose up, and he turned back around, knowing it would stay that way for some time.

Despite everything they'd been through, and the dangers that could still be waiting up ahead, Alex couldn't help but gawk from his cramped perch in the backseat. Though his mom traveled for work all the time, Alex's shaky health had always made going along too big a risk. He'd always dreamed of being able to go to cool, far-off places.

Now London sprawled all around them: an unfamiliar city full of fresh names and new sights. As the car skirted around a crowded public square, Alex eyed a winged statue and read the sign: Piccadilly Circus. The buildings on one side were fronted with neon billboards, and on the other with ancient stone. It seemed half Times Square and half medieval metropolis.

A few more quick turns and suddenly they were pulling up to a grand stone building that towered above them, as large as a city block.

"The British Museum," Ren said in a reverent whisper. "My dad always talks about this place."

Alex nodded. His mom had, too. It was beautiful.

Aditi pulled up to a gate in the tall iron fence and slowed to a halt as she reached a little guard booth. She lowered her window and flashed an ID badge at the guard, who didn't bother to look at it. "All good, then, Glenn?" she said to him.

"Near as I can tell!" he said, waving her through.

Alex was glad to see the security, but Aditi clearly wasn't satisfied. She pulled the little car to a stop and parked it near the fence. The overheated engine sounded like a deflating balloon as she switched it off. "Right!" she said. "Out we go. Quickly!"

They all piled out of the car — and into the one next to it. It was a dark blue sedan, as generic as the museum car was distinctive and, mercifully, quite a bit larger. Even better, this one didn't have their destination painted on the side. "In, in, in!" called Aditi. "Luggage in the boot."

"The what?" said Luke.

Aditi answered by popping open the trunk. Barely a minute after they'd pulled into the employee lot, they pulled back out again. Glenn gave them a slightly baffled wave and then went back to his paper and tea.

As they drove away, Alex took a quick look back through the tall iron bars. He felt a wave of relief: This lady knew what she was doing after all. The little car was clearly visible from the street. Its cheery red-and-white paint scheme called out like a billboard to any thugs, cult operatives, or other interested parties. *We're in here, dummies*, it seemed to say.

"Now, then, Luke," said Aditi, "where is this camp of yours?"

And just like that, they were off to their first destination.

The blue sedan was barely out of sight when Glenn rose from his seat in the security booth once more.

"Delivery!" called a large, moon-faced man leaning out the driver's-side window.

Glenn eyeballed the van. It was a little ragged by museum standards. Clearly not delivering any priceless artifacts. *Maybe food*, thought the guard, *or toilet valves*. "What's in the back?" he said.

"Oh, just supplies 'n' such," said Liam. "Got all 'at paperwork right 'ere."

Liam's head disappeared back into the van, and when Glenn leaned in for a closer look, Liam was waiting. He grabbed the back of Glenn's head with one powerful hand as the other one shot up toward the guard's neck. The gleaming metal point of a large hypodermic needle sank deep into the soft, pale flesh of Glenn's neck. For a moment, he twitched and jerked and tried to pull away, but as Liam pushed the plunger down with his thumb, the guard fell still.

The Order was making its presence felt.

Bumps in the Night

"Home again, home again, jiggety-jog!" called Dr. Aditi, bringing the car to a lurching halt.

Ren's eyes snapped open in the backseat. She and Alex had both conked out after they'd dropped off Luke, unable to overcome the combined effects of jet lag, sleep debt, and head trauma. She sat up and peered between the seats. The first thing she saw was a large blue sign affixed to the brick wall in front of them:

THE CAMPBELL COLLECTION

OF EGYPTIAN ANTIQUITIES

"You'll be staying here for a while," said Aditi. Ren liked the way she talked, dispensing her crisply accented words like a banker peeling new bills off a money roll. "Safer than the museum at the moment," she continued, "though there's been plenty of *activity* here, as well."

Ren set her wheelie bag down on the parking lot pavement and looked up. The London sky was gray and gloomy, just like in a movie. She bounced her bag briskly up onto the curb. "What is this place?" she said to Aditi's back.

"The Campbell used to be a private collection, but now it's a sort of satellite to the British Museum," said Aditi.

Ren looked up at the tall, skinny building in front of her: It looked like a bit of an "antiquity" itself. The paint was beginning to peel on the old-fashioned wood-framed windows, and here and there she saw little gaps in the bricks. At the very top, she saw an old chimney leaning away from the building at an angle that looked unsafe. It reminded her of a tall, broken-down old man, tipping his cap to no one.

"I've arranged rooms for you two here," Aditi added.

Here? thought Ren. *In this creaky old place?*

Inside, the Campbell Collection was cool and quiet. An old man named Somers led them to their rooms and gave them a heavy iron skeleton key for the front door. Ren wasn't sure if Somers was his first name or his last name, or if he was the caretaker, curator, or something else entirely. But Aditi said they could trust him, and that was a relief. They came to a stop outside two low, narrow doors at the end of a top-floor hallway.

"Here you are," he said in a deep, scratchy voice. "The old servants' quarters."

He turned the doorknob in front of him with long, bony fingers. It opened with a brisk click, revealing a tiny room with one narrow bed, a table, chair, dresser, lamp, and nothing else.

"Both rooms are the same," said Somers. "Doesn't much matter which one you choose."

Ren looked at Alex. "I'll take this one," she said and wheeled her bag inside.

On the floor next to the bed she saw a small metal basin and a water jug: a chamber pot, like in a Charles Dickens novel. *Please let this place have a real bathroom*, she thought. She felt like she'd taken off from New York in the twenty-first century and landed in London in the nineteenth. Once again she got the sense of being ever so slightly separated from reality. Mummies and magic will do that, but sometimes even the normal things seemed off to her now.

She thumped her bag down as Somers opened the next door for Alex. "I'll let you two get some rest," Aditi called from the hall. "Be back in the afternoon!"

Ren could hear Alex protesting in the hallway. He wanted to get started now.

"I think you've had quite enough excitement for one morning," countered Aditi, her footsteps already heading toward the stairwell.

Ren took out her phone and looked at the time. Still too early to call her parents in New York. She pressed her hand into her bed, gauging its firmness. She thought maybe she'd take Aditi's advice and get some rest. Then Alex ducked his head into her room.

"Hey, Ren," he said. "Where's that newspaper?"

And she knew she wouldn't be getting that nap after all.

They spent that first, jet-lagged day doing what they could from the Campbell. Ren got a little burst of energy when they divided up the tasks, since that was the kind of thing she liked to do.

"Okay," she said, "I'll go online and look for potential Death Walkers. Missing mummies, busted sarcophagi . . ." She glanced over at the picture of the wrapped hand in the paper, now lying open on her bed. "Anything tightly wrapped and very evil."

"Cool," said Alex. "I'll check out the collection here. See if there's anything useful. I think I saw a Book of the Dead display on the way in."

Ren had seen it, too, but it was just one panel. The full copy at the Met had taken up an entire wall: two hundred spells spread across papyrus scrolls and linen mummy wrappings. "I guess we only need one spell," she said. "If it's the right one."

That was her job. Find out who the Death Walker was in life, so they'd know which spell would work on it in death.

But as the day wore on, Ren's eyes got heavy and fuzzy as she bumped into one dead end after another. She couldn't find any reports of mummies missing from the British Museum — and it was the kind of thing that people usually noticed.

She looked up every ancient corpse listed in their collection online — and even the ones on the websites of a few of the smaller collections around town. None of them seemed especially evil: minor nobility, a high priest here and there, and even one royal accountant. *The Stung Man sounded like a Death Walker,* she thought sleepily, *but the Accountant?*

Alex returned after a thorough search, reporting that the Book of the Dead downstairs was just "a few scraps from the beginning," the Campbell's one human mummy was still very much in residence, and Aditi had called to say she wouldn't be back that day because something had happened at the big museum.

What neither of them knew was that, later that night, something was going to happen at the little one, too.

Puhh-THUUMMP!

There it was again. Alex looked around the dark confines of his little room. It was the middle of the night, and strange noises were coming from somewhere in the closed museum.

Whup-WHUMMP!

Farther away and louder? Closer and quieter? Alex couldn't tell. He sat up in the narrow wooden bed and flicked on the small lamp on the bedside table. He checked the corners of the room. Nothing. He exhaled.

Puhl–TIKKK!

The sharpest sound yet . . . Was it coming from the hallway?

"Hey, Ren," he ventured, turning to face the wall. "That you?"

Silence for a second and then: "No . . . I thought it was you!"

The walls were thin enough that they could have a conversation at more or less normal volume.

"Hallway?" said Alex.

Praang!

They were both quiet for a moment, analyzing what they'd just heard.

"It's coming from downstairs, I think," said Ren. "I think the floors are as thin as the walls."

"Okay," said Alex. "Meet you out there?"

"Yeah, just a second."

Alex threw back the thin covers and surveyed his outfit. Pajama pants and a King Tut T-shirt his mom had brought back from a trip to Egypt. *Good enough*, he figured. If it was a would-be Order assassin making that noise — or the mummy from the second floor — the only item that would matter was the amulet around his neck. He pulled the room's one chair out from under the door handle. Through the wall, he heard Ren doing the same thing. The doors of the old servants' quarters didn't lock.

He wrapped his left hand around the scarab and felt his pulse quicken, his senses sharpen. He pushed his door open and ducked his head out into the hallway. The only light came from a red EXIT sign above the staircase at the far end of the hall.

He saw Ren duck her head out a few feet away, her dark, not-quite-shoulder-length hair edged in red. She turned to look at him —

WHOMP!

The sound was louder out here, and he saw her eyes go wide with fear.

"What *is* that?" she whispered.

"I don't know," he mouthed.

Quietly, carefully, they both stepped out into the hallway. Ren was fully dressed, her sneakers tied in fresh, impeccable bunny ears. Alex looked down at his own bare feet.

He squeezed his amulet a little tighter. He thought maybe he could sense something, small and subtle, like movement at the very edge of his vision. "Only one way to find out," he said, lifting his chin toward the old stairwell.

Ren hesitated and then whispered, "Okay."

BWWAACKK!

The sound echoed up the stairwell. Ren pointed a single finger down toward the floor, and he nodded. They were on the fourth floor of the narrow building, and the latest sound seemed to be coming from the third.

Alex edged forward and took the lead. Grim images of what might be down there filled his mind, but he pushed against his fear as if he were wading into icy cold waves at the shore. A small part of him even hoped it was someone from the death cult. The familiar refrain flashed through his thoughts: Find The Order, find my mom.

He walked straight toward the garish red glow of the EXIT sign and the dark mouth of the stairwell beyond.

"Oh No"

As they descended the dark stairwell, a symphony of small creaks and groans played on the old wooden stairs. The next loud noise made them jump.

WAHhwhuuMMPPP!

The sound echoed up the stairwell. *Closer*, thought Alex. *Definitely closer.* His imagination force-fed him images he did not want to see: *the beefy Order operative looming above him, slamming the suitcase down; the empty eye sockets of the shriveled mummy on the second floor; the horrors he'd seen back home.*

Ren's smartphone glowed softly in the stairway, Dr. Aditi a touchscreen away. Alex remembered her voice from the brief phone call that day, distracted and upset. She didn't say what had happened at the British Museum, but he could tell it was bad. Even if they called her right now, he realized as they reached the third-floor landing, there was a good chance she'd arrive too late.

PRRaaaKKK!

The noise rang out in the dark. It sounded like stone or bone. It also sounded like it was coming from the next room.

"You ready?" he whispered.

"Guess so," answered Ren as they crept toward the low archway leading to a small side room.

In addition to the glow of the EXIT signs, there was a faint glow coming in through the windows, and here and there small bulbs illuminated display cases. A larger bulb washed the flat green surface of a six-thousand-year-old mudstone paint palette. The assortment of lights spawned a web of shadows. The Campbell was quiet during the day but downright spooky at night. They were almost at the archway now. His eyes brushed past a sign that read GALLERY XI: ANIMALS IN THE AFTERLIFE. They could hear another, softer sound coming from within: the raspy, irregular scratch of something being dragged across the wooden floor.

"Wait," hissed Ren, stopping in front of a small fire extinguisher.

Gladly, thought Alex. He gripped his amulet in one sweaty palm. The old floor felt cool and rough against his bare feet. He watched as the concentration line appeared between Ren's eyebrows. She carefully sized up the clasps in the dim light and then, with three quick movements, removed the fire extinguisher from its mount.

Wuh-PAAPPP!

The volume removed all doubt: The sound was coming from the next room — and coming toward them!

A scritch like fingernails scraping stone grew louder, just inside the archway. The sound was inhuman — that was no Order operative, Alex realized. What if it was something far worse? What if the Death Walker they were looking for was looking for them? They weren't prepared yet for a fight like that.

He glanced back at Ren. It was too late to hide, but could they run? As he saw Ren look down and freeze in fear, he understood: It was too late for that, too.

Holding his breath, he followed her gaze:

A pointy tail flicking back and forth.

Four stick-thin legs . . .

It was a creature with the body of a small animal, but its head was covered in a tangled mass of fractured wood and bent metal, which it was dragging backward through the archway. The strange creature was covered in . . .

"Oh no," said Alex as the little beast dragged itself out of the shadows and into the weakly lit room.

"Is that . . ." Ren began.

"Yeah," said Alex, backing slowly away. "It's mummy wrapping."

The creature paid no mind to the voices behind it, just continued dragging its burden across the floor. After a few more steps, it swung its neck hard against the base of the archway. The wood and metal slammed against the wall with astounding force. The noise rang through the room, and the friends jumped back another step.

"It must've tried to back out of its case and gotten stuck," said Ren, lowering the fire extinguisher. "It's trying to get its head out."

Alex loosened his grip on the amulet. The thing wasn't attacking; it was trapped. The busted remains of a display case wreathed its head. The electric cord of a display lamp wound through the wreckage and wrapped around the creature's neck.

"What *is* it?" said Ren. "Did they have Chihuahuas back then?"

Alex shook his head and watched the creature's long tail flick from side to side as it resumed its backward march. It was nearly hairless and half-wrapped in old linen; it was disoriented from its long sleep and trapped in the remains of its own case. But he knew exactly what it was.

"Cat," he said. "Sometimes they mummified cats. To take with them to the afterlife."

The cat mummy was closer now. Alex took another step back, but Ren took a step forward. "Poor thing," she said.

"Really?" said Alex, but he knew she was serious when he saw the familiar line appear on her brow.

"I may not like all this magic and creepy dead stuff much," she said, "but I do like cats." Ren darted forward and knelt down next to the little creature. "Easy, easy," she said. "Pretty kitty. Don't smash me."

Alex could see her fingers trembling as she worked to unfasten an upside-down clasp and untangle the remains of the electric cord.

58

"Careful!" he said, not only remembering the force with which the creature had swung its case but also eyeing its needle-like claws.

But the ex-cat had frozen at the first touch and seemed to be willing to wait. Did it know Ren was trying to help, or did it just think she was petting it?

"Almost done, little kitty," said Ren. "Almost free."

A few tugs and twists later, Ren stood up.

Slowly, tentatively, the little cat tugged its head back. Two large, pointed ears popped free from the wreckage. It turned and looked up at them with eyes that glowed green in the dim room. For just a second, they had a clear view of it — a skinny half-wrapped cat with iridescent eyes.

"It's sort of . . ." Alex began.

"Cute," confirmed Ren.

And it was, in a naked mole rat sort of way. Still, it was weird and spooky — especially in the half-dark room.

"I'll get the lights," said Alex, reaching not for the wall but his amulet.

They clicked on above them, flooding the room with light. Alex and Ren blinked a few times, and when they looked back down at the floor, the creepy-cute cat was gone.

Now that, thought Alex, *really* was *spooky*.

"Where did it go?" sputtered Ren. "How?"

"It's a mummy cat, Ren," said Alex. "Don't try to make sense of it."

The cat's path was clearly marked with periodic dings and

dents along the wall. They followed it back to its source: an overturned table and a puddle of glass.

"Somers is not going to be happy about this," said Ren.

Alex pictured the old man's flyaway white hair and the dark circles under his wrinkle-wrapped eyes. "I don't think Somers has been happy since, like, 1963."

He knelt down and carefully plucked a brass information plaque out of the broken glass. He stood up, turned it over, and read it:

PAI-EN-INMAR, SACRED CAT

FROM THE TEMPLE OF BASTET

BUBASTIS, C. 1730 BC

Alex knew all about Bastet: Part protector and part predator, the cat-headed goddess was both revered and feared in ancient Egypt. His mom had always wanted to get a cat and name it Bastet. And though she'd never said so, Alex knew why she hadn't: He'd always been more than enough to care for.

Ren stepped over and plucked the plaque from his hands, snapping him back to reality.

"Mine," she said.

He didn't argue. She'd definitely earned it.

They cleaned up as best they could and headed back upstairs.

Back in his room, Alex fell into a fitful sleep as the adrenaline surge faded. But he did wake briefly just before dawn, and in those few blurry moments, he could've sworn he heard soft, small steps out in the hallway.

Office Work

Alex woke up in a dark mood the next morning, and he stayed in one as Dr. Aditi drove them to the British Museum. His thoughts were grim and determined as the city slid by his window. They pulled into the same side lot as the day before, but Alex noticed that a different guard was on duty, and this one seemed much less relaxed.

That was fine. He was less relaxed, too. He couldn't believe how much time he'd wasted already, spinning his wheels at the Campbell while his mom was held captive somewhere. The idea that she might be suffering — never far from his thoughts — jutted into his mind like an iceberg piercing the hull of a ship.

The three hurried into the staff entrance and up toward Aditi's office. Alex quickly eyed the massive museum: huge rooms, sleek new display cases brimming with invaluable artifacts, and already full of visitors. It was the exact opposite of the sleepy old Campbell Collection, but a British brother to the Met. He looked over and saw Ren gawking at it all and felt like shouting at her: *We're not tourists!*

They whisked through a large, impressive atrium and past the shuttered Egyptian exhibits. Alex read a sign at the entrance: THIS GALLERY IS IN THE COURSE OF REARRANGE-MENT. WE APOLOGISE FOR ANY INCONVENIENCE. He thought of the "rearrangements" at the Met: everything from restless mummies to ancient diseases.

Dr. Aditi's office was a mess, papers and folders everywhere, the blinds hanging lopsided. Alex took it all in at a glance. "Someone broke in, didn't they?" he guessed. *Is that why we wasted an entire day?* he wanted to add.

He and Ren took seats in the two chairs in front of the cluttered desk and their host took a seat behind it. Ren opened her notebook and awaited the reply. To Alex, this "junior internship" was just a cover story, but he was pretty sure it was more than that to Ren. It would be a sweet credential for the high-stakes demolition derby of high school admission in Manhattan. His friend's open notebook and new, blue, first-day-of-school dress were all the confirmation he needed.

Dr. Aditi glanced over to confirm the door was closed, let out a long, tired breath, and began. "Yes," she said. "We have a guard in the hospital, injected with horse tranquilizers, apparently. Lucky to be alive. All these folders on top of my desk were on the floor. All the files inside them, many confidential, were outside them."

Ren scribbled furiously in her notebook. "The men from the airport?" she asked.

"Presumably," said Aditi.

"What were they looking for?"

"That's the question," said Aditi. "The only folder I'm sure they took was the one on the Lost Spells. The official one, anyway. My private file is on the computer, hidden behind a few extra passwords. Don't think they got through."

Alex pictured the crew of bone-breakers from the airport: not exactly hacker types. But something still didn't make sense. "But why would they want our info on the Lost Spells? They have the Spells. They stole them from the Met when they got my mom."

"Perhaps they're wondering what exactly it is they have," said Aditi. She paused. "But we have to at least consider the possibility they don't have the Spells."

His head swam at the implications. "But . . ." he began, but then he shook it off. "Fine, whatever," he said, not bothering to hide the annoyance in his voice. He didn't agree, but he was sick of talking about this stuff. "We need to get moving, anyway."

"Excuse me?" said Dr. Aditi, looking across her cluttered desk at him.

Alex returned the look. "We need to get moving. Like, now."

"Do you think you're in charge here?" she said.

"No," he admitted, though he wished he was. "But it's pretty *obvious*. We need to get out there and find out what's going on. That's why I'm —" He caught himself a little too late and looked over at Ren. "I mean, that's why we're here, right?"

Now they were both giving him looks.

"I'll be blunt," said Dr. Aditi. "You are here" — she leaned forward in her chair — "because you have both done this before, and you, Alex, are the only one who can use the scarab. We will need it if there is a Death Walker here — and it certainly seems that there is."

"And we need the Book of the Dead, too," said Ren.

Alex stared at her, annoyed that she was trying to score internship points while he was trying to get things moving. She had a point, though. The little display at the Campbell was no help. Dr. Aditi began to answer, but he cut her off. "Do you have one here?" he said. "Can we get it?"

She looked at him and made him wait a moment before responding. "This is the British Museum," she said. "It can be arranged — at least a scroll or two. But first we must learn who or what we are dealing with."

"So we'll know which spell to use," added Ren, and Alex wanted to tell her to knock it off already. He glanced down at her open notebook and saw that she was making a list: three numbered items, but he couldn't quite read them.

"Precisely," said Aditi.

"Yeah, *congratulations* for telling us what we already know," he said.

"Don't be a jerk," said Ren.

"Then don't be a teacher's pet," he said. She glared at him, but he was already turning back toward Aditi. "All any of that means is that we need to get out there and start looking."

"*First* we need information," said Aditi evenly.

The more overheated Alex got, the more her calmness bothered him. He began drumming his fingers on his thigh.

"And we should start by reviewing what we already have," she continued, ignoring Alex's eye roll. "We will '*get out there*' when we absolutely need to. You are still twelve, after all, and in my charge."

Alex slumped slightly in his chair. His fingers stopped. He couldn't argue himself any older.

Aditi reached into the top drawer of her desk and pulled out two manila envelopes. "For now, I've printed up a file for each of you," she said. "Everything that's happened here to date. Look it over. See if anything rings a bell from the last time. I'll set you up in a spare office."

Alex couldn't believe it: *A Death Walker on the loose, red rain, his mom missing, The Order running wild, and she wants us to spend the day* doing homework? He looked over at Ren, hoping for support, but she was eagerly reaching for her folder.

They needed to know who this new Death Walker was, but that wasn't going to be in the newspapers. It's not like they'd *interviewed* the thing.

As Aditi leaned forward to hand him his folder, the thin gold chain around her neck slipped out from under her collar. Alex stared. *Would it be an amulet on the chain? What shape would it have? What powers?* But instead, he caught a quick glimpse of a green gem, the size of a pencil eraser. He couldn't believe it: *She doesn't even have an amulet.*

He took the folder and sank back into his seat. *Just great,* he thought.

They followed Aditi to the spare office, and Ren had just one question for her on the way. "Are all the mummies still, you know, here?"

"It's in the folder," said Aditi. "But yes. One of them is getting a little . . . fidgety, but they're all present and accounted for."

When they arrived, it was more of a small conference room than an office, but it didn't matter. Alex had no intention of staying long. He read enough to get the idea and then flipped through the rest. Ren read diligently, without comment. Alex could tell she was annoyed at him. He didn't know why. Everything he'd said had been total common sense. *Well, except maybe the teacher's pet thing*, he thought.

Finally, she sat back, pulled two printouts out of the stack, and began copying information down into her notebook.

"What?" he said.

"This is really interesting," she said.

"Yeah?" he said.

"It's these two," she said, tipping the printouts toward him.

"I, uh, I didn't get to those."

She didn't seem surprised. "It's about the grave robberies," she said. "They were both at the same place."

Now we're getting somewhere, he thought. "Is it far?"

"It's in the north of the city," she said, reaching for a third printout. "But probably not too far by train."

Alex's right knee began pumping up and down under the table. "Let's get out of here," he said. "Let's check it out."

The Investigation Begins

The hardest part of sneaking out of the museum was convincing Ren to do it. After that, it was a piece of cake. Big museums were pretty much the same on either side of the Atlantic, and they blew through the offices with their well-practiced "staff kids" walks. They knew from the Met that no one ever asked for ID on the way out.

They hit the sidewalk in no time flat.

"Okay, where were the robberies?" said Alex, in full-on Go Mode now.

"Highgate Cemetery," said Ren, a note of caution in her voice.

Alex got the impression that was supposed to mean something to him. He shook his head and made a *ya got me* expression.

"It's super famous," said Ren, as if that might ring a bell. "Really old and creepy?"

Alex shrugged. "How do we get there?"

Ren flipped to the maps at the back of her guidebook as they headed down the sidewalk. Alex saw a forest of mint green Post-it notes sticking out from the pages.

"From here we go to . . ." she began. Then she looked up, her eyes wide. "Goodge Street!"

Alex pumped his fist. The name of that Underground stop had been one of the clues that led them to London in the first place, after they'd found it on a scrap of burnt paper in The Order's underground lair in New York.

Ren held up her hand for a high five, but Alex's phone chirped with an incoming text and he left her hanging. They both froze as he checked the screen.

"Is it Dr. Aditi?" said Ren.

"Just Luke again," he said, flicking his phone to silent. Ren did the same with hers: standard procedure when there was spy work to be done.

"Remember," said Ren. "Just a quick look around and then we go straight back to the Campbell and tell Dr. Aditi we went back to study the folders. Which you should."

"Sure," said Alex. She was better at cover stories than he was, anyway. His had always been the same — too sick — and they had always been true. Not now. He had energy, and he had direction.

Goodge Street was on the Northern Line, a short walk away. They reached the station, bought their fare cards, and took the elevator down far below street level. "This is a lot deeper than the New York subway," said Ren. "I don't really like it."

"Why not?" said Alex as the lift doors opened and they exited into tunnels lined in clean white tile.

"It's like a tomb," she said.

Alex nodded. He'd also been thinking about tombs a lot lately. He felt his scarab amulet bounce against his chest as they headed toward the train. The scarab was the symbol of the Returner, a traveler between the world of the living and the world of the dead. He'd been in both worlds now, and it was just starting to occur to him:

Maybe he still was.

Highgate

They exited the Archway station and started up the long slope of Highgate Hill. The neighborhood got cleaner and quieter as they began to climb, smudged storefronts giving way to rows of pleasant town houses on either side of the street.

Alex wanted to head straight for the cemetery, but Ren insisted on taking a detour to look at some of the spots where people had disappeared. Alex moped a few steps behind as they took a road heading across the hill.

Before long, they stood on the sidewalk gazing across a tiny lawn at the house of the first two missing persons. It looked to be a two-family home, but a scrap of blue-and-white police tape still stuck to one of the door frames left no doubt which unit the boys had disappeared from.

"Two brothers, seventeen and eighteen," said Ren, glancing down at a copy of a newspaper story. "Police thought maybe they'd just run away."

"Until the next one," said Alex.

It didn't take them long to find that one. The houses weren't exactly neighbors, but they were both near the bottom of the hill. They knew all about this missing person already.

"An eleven-year-old boy . . . Robbie," said Ren.

Alex nodded. "The couple from the airport . . . their nephew," he said. He could still see their eyes: wide and worried and rimmed with the dark circles of too many sleepless nights. They reminded him of how his mom had looked when his own health had begun to fail.

He shook his head hard, trying to dislodge the image. It was an old habit, and it had only gotten worse lately. Ren pretended not to notice, as usual. Instead, she flipped through her folder for the details. "He was on the ground floor," she said. "They found the window open the next morning."

"Broken?" said Alex.

"Nope," said Ren. "Opened from the inside."

Alex's eyes found the bedroom window and his blood ran cold. He'd seen a hyena-masked Order operative named Al-Dab'u controlling an entire construction crew. He'd seen a police detective Todtman had brainwashed. And now a boy had opened his own window and climbed out into the arms of the night. Whoever took these people — The Order or the Walker — he was pretty sure they ended up in the same place. He needed to know where that was.

"Let's get to the cemetery," he said.

"Well, there was another guy who disappeared," said Ren. She pointed. "Sort of over and down, just past the bottom of the hill."

Alex didn't want to go backward. "It's just going to be another stupid house," he said.

"Houses aren't stupid," said Ren.

"Well, they aren't smart," he snapped. "And they're not going to start flapping their doors and talking."

"Why are you being so mean today?" said Ren.

"Why do you think?" he said.

Ren mumbled something under her breath, but he didn't catch it.

"Which way to Highgate Cemetery?" he said.

She pointed to the very top of the hill.

Morbid thoughts slipped into Alex's head as he began an uphill slog that would have been impossible for him a few weeks earlier. Soon he picked up his pace and took the lead. He knew they were getting closer to the old graveyard now.

He could feel his amulet getting warmer with each step.

Ren, on the other hand, felt a chill spreading up her spine. They were heading toward Highgate Cemetery. Older than some states back in the US, the place had been packed since World War I. Nearly a century of mossy overgrowth and benign neglect had left it famously spooky and reportedly haunted.

"There it is," said Alex.

"I see it," she said. "Slow down."

A high iron fence surrounded the sprawling west cemetery, the older section — and the one where the robberies had taken place. It was closed now, except for a daily tour. Even if they managed to get in, they'd be the only ones inside. The only ones alive, anyway.

Alex didn't slow down at all, and Ren struggled to match his longer stride. Finally, the entrance came into view. There was a large stone complex with an iron fence extending from it in either direction and a heavy iron gate in the middle. To Ren, it looked less like the entrance to a cemetery than the entrance to a castle.

Alex exhaled loudly and stared at it. She knew what it looked like to him: just another obstacle in his search. He was being a jerk — again — but at least she felt like she understood that part a little better now. She wasn't as close with her parents as Alex was with his mom, but she was surprised by how much she already missed them.

Still, she thought as they crossed the street, *Alex could be nicer. He isn't the only one making sacrifices.* She glanced up at the silent cemetery. *And he certainly isn't the only one taking risks.*

There didn't seem to be anyone around as they approached the gate. "Do we, like, knock?" said Alex.

A door opened in the stone building to the right of the gate. "May I help you?"

If you spend any time at all around museums — and Ren had spent a lot — there is a certain kind of older lady who becomes very familiar. Polite, polished, confident, and impeccably dressed. The very embodiment of this sort of lady stood before them now. She could have been their queen.

"Ah, little ones!" she said. "Gave me a fright. Things are a bit . . . unsettled here lately. I'm sorry, but you've missed the tour. Come back tomorrow, 1:45 sharp." She paused to look around and frowned slightly. "And bring your parents, won't you?"

"Uhhh, we . . ." said Alex.

Ren's eyes went wide with alarm. Alex was smart in his own way — he certainly knew a ton about ancient Egypt. But he was trying to think on the fly now, and this did not always end well.

"We're relatives?" he continued. "Of one of the, um, deceased? Inside?"

Interesting, thought Ren. The lady seemed to think the same thing, because she allowed him to continue. Alex seemed encouraged.

"Yes!" he said. "We've come all the way from America — it's our last day here! We were hoping to . . . maybe . . ."

"You want to visit the grave?" volunteered the volunteer.

Alex nodded enthusiastically.

"I see," said the lady. "And what is the name of your relative?"

"He's English," Alex began. Ren knew he was stalling. "His name is, um, London?"

Ren winced.

"London?" said the lady.

"Yes," said Alex. "London, um, Penny . . . feather?"

"London Pennyfeather," said the lady evenly, as if weighing the words.

Alex gave her a wide, defensive smile.

"I'm sorry," said the woman. "I don't think so."

She turned on the heel of her stylishly functional leather boot and disappeared back into the little stone building. "Come back tomorrow!" she called a moment before the door slammed behind her.

Ren looked from the freshly closed door to the still closed gate, then at Alex. "London Pennyfeather?" she said.

Alex looked down sheepishly. "Yeah," he managed. "Good old Great-uncle Pennyfeather."

Ren chuckled and Alex just shook his head ruefully. It felt good to share a joke again.

But then the smile fell from Alex's face and the determined set of his jaw returned. The change was too sudden for Ren to match, and the smile was still stranded on her face as Alex reached into his shirt and removed his amulet.

"I can get us in," he said.

Egyptian Avenue

Alex was expecting a click, but instead he got a *Ka-LUNKK!*

It wasn't the first lock he'd opened with his amulet, but it was definitely the largest — and the oldest by a solid century.

"Ready?" he said, looking back to find Ren stuffing her folder back in her messenger bag. She nodded. Study time was over. It was time for the test.

Alex released his amulet and gave the big gate a push.

Gate: *KkREEEEEEEEAAK!*

Door: *THUNNK!*

Lady: "Stop right now!"

Alex and Ren made a break for it. Their feet slapped loudly on the stone tiles of the courtyard, and Ren's folder fell out of her bag.

"Oh no!" she blurted.

Alex turned and saw loose papers spilling across the stone

and the woman closing in on Ren. "Come on!" he called. "It's just printouts!"

Ren resumed running, and she and Alex quickly pulled away. They reached the edge of the courtyard, and Alex felt a sense of crazy elation as he took the old stone steps two at a time. For twelve years, he'd been the sick kid, the frail kid. He couldn't remember the last time he made it through a full gym class.

And now? He felt the wind push his hair back as he ran. *For all it cost*, he thought, *coming back from the dead definitely has its benefits*. He imagined his mom, alone with him in that hospital room, reciting the spell that gave him this new life. *The last thing she did for me* . . . He shook his head hard, on the fly.

Old graves sprouted on either side of a central path, large stone monuments with moss climbing the sides and lichen clinging to the tops. Death and decay and life all at once.

"This way!" Alex called to Ren, a few feet back. They switched directions without breaking stride and headed down a muddy side path. Carefully planted trees had gone rogue over the years and now sprang up all around them.

Twenty yards in, they stopped.

"Think we lost her," he said, huffing and puffing.

"We lost her," Ren began, pausing for a gulp of air, "thirty feet after we found her." Another huff. "She didn't make it out of the courtyard."

They grabbed a few more lungfuls and then straightened up and started walking.

"I can't believe I dropped my folder," said Ren, grimacing.

"Just printouts of news stories and stuff," said Alex, and he was mostly right. Except for the letter at the end: the one on Dr. Aditi's official museum letterhead.

"Anyway," said Ren. "I think I remember where the first disturbance was."

They walked on, looking at the elaborate sculptures on the graves: angels, crosses, and more surprising shapes. Many of the monuments listed the occupations, and even the addresses, of the deceased. Others provided clues to their lives.

"I'll bet that was his pet," said Ren, pointing to a sad stone dog, curled up at the base of a tombstone.

"Bet he was a carriage driver," said Alex, pointing to a large stone carriage on top of another. "It reminds me of Egypt."

"Because of the, like, coffin-y things?" said Ren, nodding at the nearest one. The bodies here weren't buried. They were interred in stone boxes aboveground.

Alex looked at one. The resemblance to an Egyptian sarcophagus was unmistakable. "Yeah, and just, I don't know, the idea that you *can* take it with you." He pointed back at the stone dog. "That guy's kind of like your new friend, you know?"

"That little cat gave me the creeps!" said Ren, but with a small smile on her face. Then she stopped and pointed up the path. "There's the first one."

The torn remains of blue-and-white police tape flapped idly in the breeze, a dead giveaway. They walked over slowly.

"Orvath Bridgers," said Alex, reading the raised letters on the large stone box. "Sounds like two clothing companies got married."

The top of the monument had been lifted back into place, but Alex eyed the fresh cement filling the jagged line that ran down its center. Hundreds of pounds, but it had been knocked off and shattered like a plate to get at what was inside — or who was.

"It says Orvath was a goldsmith," said Ren.

Alex read the line, GOLDSMITH TO THE RICH AND ROYAL, and sized up the expensive monument. "If you thought you could take it with you," he said, "what would a famous goldsmith take?"

They headed up the hill toward the next grave, Ren leading the way and both of them turning this new puzzle piece over in their minds.

"They robbed graves in ancient Egypt, too," said Ren.

"Yeah, but if they caught you back then, they cut off your hand."

"Gross," said Ren, but then she had another thought. "It's like the Crown Jewels. The gold, I mean. It's fancy, just like with . . ."

80

"The Stung Man," said Alex, remembering. "Like how he decorated his tomb with stolen loot, nice things."

"Yeah, but it's more than nice things this time," said Ren. "This is treasure."

Alex nodded. Treasure stolen from a grave . . . "Let's check out the next one."

They continued up the slope and turned a gentle corner on the path.

"Here it is," said Ren. "And you thought this place reminded you of Egypt before."

Alex couldn't believe what he was seeing, not how strange it was, but how familiar. A massive stone archway towered above them, with columns carved on either side. *It may be balanced on an English hillside*, thought Alex, *but the style is all Nile.*

"They call it Egyptian Avenue," said Ren, earning her extra credit.

Alex could see why immediately. "It's a tomb front," he said, noticing the carved lotus flowers. "I mean, you could plop this thing down in the Egyptian wing at the Met and no one would look twice. The size, the style, the columns . . . everything."

"Not everything," said Ren, pointing at the twin rows of shadowy doorways that lay beyond the archway. "These tombs are aboveground."

They ventured slowly under the archway and into the avenue. The linked crypts loomed on either side of them, their worn stone facades speckled with moss and age, their heavy doors painted black as night.

"I don't know," said Ren, falling a few steps behind. "Maybe we should come back with Dr. Aditi . . ."

"What good would that do?" said Alex dismissively. "She doesn't even have an amulet."

"Neither do I," Ren said under her breath, but Alex was already talking again.

"Here it is," he said.

In front of him, one of the black doors hung open, half off its hinges. He scanned the facade. "There's no name on this one, no nothing," he said. "Did the articles say who it was?"

Ren mumbled her response, her eyes fixed on the darkness within. "No. Said the records burned up in World War II."

"That's weird," said Alex, taking another step forward and craning his neck to look inside. The thin slice of gray light coming through the broken door revealed three large ceramic jars. Alex had seen ones just like them at the Met, but even in Egyptian Avenue, this seemed too much.

"Are those . . . canopic?" said Ren, standing a little farther back.

Alex shook his head. These weren't the small ceremonial jars that held the internal organs of the deceased. These were larger, more functional. "These hold provisions," he said. "For the afterlife . . . Food, drinks . . . grain, maybe . . ."

He was so engrossed that he didn't feel his amulet getting warmer against his already warm chest.

"Know a lot, boy," he heard. At least, he thought that's what it was. The voice was so thick and scratchy and raw that it was hard to tell for sure.

The friends spun toward the voice, Alex already preparing his excuses: *My great-uncle! A class project!* But it wasn't a volunteer they saw, no groundskeeper or gardener.

Alex's blood turned to ice water and his breath caught in his throat.

The man they were looking at seemed to stand nearly as high as the columns. His jaw was square and his chest was wide, and everything about him was wrong, an abomination. His outfit, once tan, by the looks of it, was now stained with thick streaks of dirt and mud. The gaudy gold jewelry encircling his neck and one wrist was tarnished by time and death. The man's skin was mottled and uneven; in some places it was stretched taut and dry, like a mummy's, and in others, it hung loose, like a pale old man's. The jagged breath slipping from his mouth spoke of damage inside. And yet, the dead man stood in broad daylight, smiling at them with time-yellowed teeth.

Alex knew immediately that it wasn't a friendly look.

It was a hungry one.

Alex reached up for his amulet, still resting lightly outside his shirt.

The thing followed the movement and caught a glimpse before Alex's hand wrapped around it.

"A scarab," he rasped, barely intelligible.

Alex hardly heard it anyway, all his attention drawn to the creature's eyes. They were like reverse stars, dots of pure black hovering in the soft gray afternoon light. He immediately, instinctively knew the truth. He'd seen that black light before. These eyes were windows into the afterlife. He looked inside, transfixed.

"Death Walker," he said, his lips forming the words almost despite him.

The Walker smiled wider. "Yyessss," he hissed.

"Alex!" called Ren from behind him. "Let's GO!"

The smile vanished and the Death Walker paced forward, heavy old boots thudding into the soft ground. One step, two steps . . . A few more and he would be close enough to grab Alex's amulet. Or throat.

But Alex was pretty fast himself these days. With a move he'd practiced a hundred times back home, and a hundred more in the park at night, his left hand squeezed the scarab as his right hand shot up.

A powerful phantom wind rose up. *The wind that comes before the rain,* a force of seasonal rebirth in Egypt. The gusts staggered this Walker, as they had the last one.

It wasn't enough to stop him, but it was enough to slow him and knock him off balance.

Alex pulled his hand back, allowing the creature to stumble into the sudden lack of resistance.

The Walker spat out half a dozen ill-formed words; the only ones Alex caught were "crush you."

Ren grabbed Alex's shoulder. "Come on!"

Alex shook her off and his hand shot up a second time. Instead of spreading his fingers wide, he pointed them tightly. It was a move born of desperation and anger, but it worked. What shot forth was not a wall of wind but a *spear* of it. The force struck the Walker on his left shoulder, and he spun back, falling to one knee.

In the few moments it took the Walker to get to his feet, Alex and Ren scrambled down the row of crypts and back onto the path. But just as Ren turned to sprint down the slope, Alex skidded to a stop. The Walker appeared under the arch.

"Alex!" Ren yelled.

But Alex didn't move, and once again, Ren reluctantly stood by her friend.

The towering Walker glared at him and Alex glared right back. "Tell me where my mom is!" he shouted.

The Walker responded to the pain in the boy's voice with a desolate and broken wheeze, a laugh like a smoker's cough.

Alex screamed back: no words, just a howl of frustration. His hand shot out, the fingers pointed again. The spear of wind whistled straight toward the Walker's head. The creature opened his mouth wide *and ate it*. The wind disappeared into a howling vacuum inside.

As Alex watched, the mouth opened wider, wider — too wide — and it blackened. Alex felt a sudden chill shoot through him, and then he felt something else: a tearing pain seemed to come from his whole body at once. He felt as if he was being *unzipped*. From head to toe: *unzipped*.

He heard a scream and turned toward its source: Ren. Just a few steps away, she was caught in the same attack. For a moment, he saw her standing there, leaning back with her heels dug in to resist the wind pulling her toward the horrible, distended mouth. And then he saw a flicker and a blur as a mirror image of his best friend slowly began to pull away from her body.

Her soul, he realized in horror.

He looked down and saw the same thing happening to him, but not in the same way. Instead of the vibrant colors peeling free from Ren's small frame, he saw a gray and misty tinge to his.

It felt like losing hope, like that poisoned-gut moment between dropping something precious and seeing it shatter. It felt like that, if the thing you'd dropped was your life and all you'd ever loved.

In that awful moment of misery, he knew he had to act. Not just for himself, but also for his friend. He could see a full second image of her head now, bending away from her body and toward the Walker.

Not much time. He felt nearly hollow inside.

He was so cold now, almost frozen. His hand was still wrapped tightly around the scarab, his head still pounding with the effort, but his right hand could no longer do anything but point toward the powerful vacuum pulling it forward.

Alex reached up with the only thing he could still control: his eyes. He flicked them up, scanning the air above the path.

He found what he was looking for.

He locked on.

Then, with all the strength and will he had left, he jerked his entire head down in one sharp nod.

The branch he'd been staring at came down with it.

KaaRRRRRAACCCCCK!

The Walker looked up in surprise, pointing his open mouth at the falling branch. Instantly, a shadow image of brown wood and green leaves tore free and disappeared down his gaping maw. A moment later, the branch crashed down on his oversized frame, knocking the foul man-thing to the ground.

Free.

Alex could feel it instantly. He gasped deeply and heard Ren doing the same next to him. He knew it wasn't just air returning to their bodies.

This time, he was the one to yell it: *"RUN!"*

They sprinted headlong down the hill. He'd been wrong to try to force this fight. He'd used the amulet to banish the first Death Walker back to the afterlife, and he knew that, somehow, he would need to do the same with this one. It was why they were in London.

But he also knew he needed more: the Book of the Dead, the right spell, the right moment — and this was not it. They needed to regroup, to plan. They needed to escape.

A loud noise echoed behind them, the sound of splintering wood, and they ran faster. He could feel his churning legs pumping heat back into his chilled body. As they descended the hillside, the gatehouse came into view. From the vantage point of the hillside, he spied something he'd missed before: a smaller side gate. It seemed a better bet than the big main gate — and he didn't want to lead that thing back to the white-haired lady.

They reached the side gate together and slammed into it, pulling it shut behind them and sprinting straight down Swain's Lane. They blew past the home of the two missing teens and didn't stop until they'd reached the small cluster of houses and shops at the bottom. Sidewalk passersby stared at them, but Alex was too worried about Ren to notice. Finally, she turned to him. Her first words were forced, squeezed out through big greedy breaths. "He must've . . . been there . . . to . . . rob another . . . grave."

Alex nodded, relieved to hear her voice again. They took a few more looks behind them, then found a bench and plopped down, collecting themselves. Alex looked up and found the sun, its cottony white outline just visible behind a bank of late-day clouds. Ren did the same thing. The warmth felt good.

Alex took out his cell phone to call Aditi, but the battery was completely drained, dead as a rock. He didn't have to wonder why or ask Ren if hers was, too. The two sat side by side and pointed their faces at the sky, their eyes closed against the pale sun, their lips purple from the cold.

Slipping Away

Dr. Aditi nodded politely as the cemetery lady let her have it.

"Yes, well, we have interns here, too, but ours know their place!"

"I'm sorry," said Aditi. "I can assure you it won't happen again."

"Yes, well, I should hope it doesn't."

Aditi played her best card: "They are Americans. Spirited, but . . ."

"That's one word for it, I suppose," said the lady. She seemed to consider something, and then let it go. "Yes, yes, they certainly were spirited. And resourceful. I have no idea how they got that lock open."

"I think they teach that in the schools over there," said Aditi.

The lady shook her head lightly and let her frown slip away.

"Yanks . . ." said Aditi, and the two shared a playful, conspiratorial smile.

The lady handed her the letter Ren had dropped, the number she'd used to call her circled in blue pen at the top. "Yours, I believe."

"Thank you," Aditi said, taking the list of emergency contact numbers. "Let me know if the museum can do anything for you here."

"Always looking for funds."

Another shared smile, then the gatekeeper headed back to her post and Aditi headed up the hillside. She sighed heavily as she topped the stone stairs at the edge of the courtyard and saw the slightly muddy main path. She was wearing entirely the wrong shoes for this.

"Alex! Ren!" she called. "Come along, please! I'm not sure it's quite . . . safe here!"

She paused to look up the path and then cast a quick, nervous glance over her shoulder. She checked her phone: still no response to her calls and texts. She pocketed it and began to trudge upward. Todtman had warned her about the kids' "initiative," as he called it. He seemed to think it was a good thing. She wasn't so sure.

"Alex!" she called. "Ren!"

No answer. She took a deep breath, steadied herself, and then continued on. She turned a gentle corner and saw a dead tree branch, split in two and lying in the middle of the walking path.

Strange, she thought. The rest of the grounds seemed well maintained.

She looked up to make sure another branch wasn't about to fall but heard heavy footsteps behind her. "Alex?" she said, turning. "Re . . ." Her voice trailed away.

The response came in a ragged rasp: "'Ello, luv."

Two strong hands clamped down on her shoulders. She tried to shake free. She struggled hard and did everything right: two hands on one wrist, find the weak point. It didn't matter. His grip was like stone.

Broken sounds spilled from the thing's lips, and this time Aditi caught only one word: "Hungry." The tussle with the Amulet Keeper had taken something out of him. He needed to feed.

Aditi glared up at the man. He was disfigured by both death and afterlife, but she recognized him just the same. "I know you," she said, and then spat in his face.

If he reaches up to wipe it away, she thought, *maybe I can slip free.*

He didn't.

His powerful hands dug into her shoulders as he opened his mouth wide and showed her oblivion. The world went cold, and the last thing she saw as her eyes turned white and her lips edged past purple was her very self, slipping away.

Alex's head was throbbing as they rode the train back to the Campbell. Using the amulet had always left him with headaches, and they seemed to be getting worse the better he got with the thing. He turned things over in his aching head as best he could. One grave robbed of gold, another containing Egyptian jars, and a Death Walker in . . . what, exactly? He wasn't entirely sure what was under all that filth, but he thought it might be . . . khaki? He pictured the man's face: damaged but pale. Replayed his words: ragged and torn but English. But how could a Death Walker — revived by the Lost Spells of ancient Egypt — be English?

He turned his tender head toward Ren. If anyone could piece this together . . . But he could see right away that she wasn't up for a debriefing. Shivering slightly in the seat next to him, she looked small and fragile.

She saw him looking. "I feel so . . . hollow," she said. She opened her mouth to clarify but couldn't find the words. She gazed down at the train floor, as if she might have dropped them there.

All Alex could do was nod. He knew exactly what she meant. He knew the ache in her heart and the dog-just-died feeling in her gut. He knew it well. His soul had slipped away before, after all. They rode on in heavy silence.

By the time they reached the Campbell Collection, his headache was a full-blown migraine. Somers was behind the front desk, and he had a single message to relay: "Aditi's looking for you. You are both in trouble."

They knew that already. There was a Death Walker in town. The two slunk upstairs, past a handful of late-day browsers. Alex rifled through his stuff for his bottle of head-ache pills, took two too many, and collapsed onto his bed.

The pressure inside his skull was unbearable. He edged toward unconsciousness, and hoped for it. Ren called through the wall, something about messages. She'd plugged in her phone.

Alex didn't answer. He'd begun the day in a dark mood. He would end it in darkness.

Fight

Alex slept straight through the evening and through most of the night, too. But after loading up at the drinking fountain before bed, he woke up with a pressing need around four a.m. All that remained of his headache was a fuzzy, unfocused feeling and a dull ache in one temple. His main problem now: The museum's restrooms were all the way down on the second floor. He eyed the chamber pot on his way out of the room, but he still had his pride.

He stumbled blearily down the dark stairwell.

He couldn't tell if his amulet felt a little hot as he passed the third floor or if he'd just been sleeping on it again. He reached his destination and pushed through the men's room door. He looked like death in the mirror under the fluorescent lights.

Flush with success, he headed back up the stairs. But he was more awake now — and the amulet did feel hot. Halfway up the last flight of stairs, the hairs on the back of his neck stood up. He wasn't alone.

Had they been followed?

A noise behind him.

He fumbled for his amulet and swung around, nearly falling.

But it was too late . . . The cat had already brushed past him, tattered linen against flannel pajama. The little mummy looked back ever so slightly as she continued up the stairs, and Alex caught a glimpse of one glowing green eye.

He clutched the railing and tried to catch his breath. "Ah . . . you scared . . . you little . . ."

He saw her again a few minutes later, already curled up outside Ren's door. *Is she asleep?* he wondered as he carefully stepped over her. *Hasn't she been doing that for, like, four thousand years?*

He closed his door, mildly creeped out but reassured by the thing's utter lack of interest in him. A door to the afterlife had opened when his mom used the Lost Spells. He was just glad that not everything that slipped out was trying to kill him. He fell back to sleep and woke up again a little after six a.m. He unplugged his phone and saw all the missed calls and unanswered texts Aditi had left the day before, laced with ones from Luke. They both wanted to know where he was. It was too early to call Aditi back, but he bit the bullet and answered the last of her texts.

He sat up and looked out the window. His head felt clear, the tenderness gone. He turned and looked at the mint-green wall. Ren was on the other side. His stone-cold amulet told him that the mummy cat had faded along with the darkness.

He wanted to wake Ren up and get an early start on things. The way he saw it, they'd already wasted an entire night. But nothing would be open yet, and he had a vague sense that maybe he hadn't been the greatest to her yesterday. He lowered his head to his pillow and let her sleep.

He passed the time turning over the new information they'd gained at the cemetery. By the time he heard a faint stirring through the wall, it was almost nine. His patience had run out and he was once again anxious to get started. Plus, it was almost time for Dr. Aditi to pick them up. But the sound faded quickly.

He raised his hand, hesitated for just a moment . . . and knocked.

Come on, he was thinking. *We've got to get going! Yeah, yesterday was rough — but that was yesterday.*

No response. He knocked again.

"WHAT?" called Ren.

Alex heard the edge in her voice, but he pushed past it. This was too important. "Time to get going!" he called.

Ren didn't answer, but he heard her thumping around loudly in her room. One shoe dropped, and then the other. He was already dressed, so he got up and walked toward his door. "Meet you in the hallway," he said.

He double-checked that the cat was gone and then took

up the same post outside her door. He had to wait for a while, but eventually the door opened.

"Uh, you look awful," he said.

"Thanks," said Ren. She ran a hand through her rumpled hair, but that wasn't the problem. Her eyes were glassy, her lips still a little too dark . . .

"I feel kinda drained," she admitted. "So sleepy."

"We're already late!"

Ren's glassy eyes went wide. "Dr. Aditi!" she said. "What time is it?"

"Almost nine thirty!"

The plan was for Aditi to pick them up a little before nine each day, on her way to the museum. They rushed down to the curb, waving at Somers, who was looking a little sleep-rumpled himself. They pushed through the front doors and into the first truly, cloudlessly sunny day since their arrival. The light hurt Alex's eyes and he blinked against it as he scanned the pavement.

But the little lot was empty except for Somers's old green shoe box of a car.

"Not here," said Ren.

"We really are in trouble," said Alex.

Ren could see Alex getting antsy again as they waited by the curb, scanning the street for familiar cars. He'd nearly gotten her killed, and all he'd had to say about it so far was "you look awful" and "you're late."

"Hey," he said. "What did the Walker's outfit look like to you?"

"His outfit?" said Ren sleepily.

"Yeah, like, what material?"

She closed her eyes and tried to remember an image she'd been trying to forget. "I don't know what material it was," she said finally, "but it had buttons."

"Yeah!" said Alex, loud enough to startle her. "They didn't button their clothing in ancient Egypt."

"You don't have to shout. We're the only ones here."

He looked at her blankly and continued. "So this one's not Egyptian, and not as old. Like, I don't know how old, but definitely in the button age."

Alex was talking fast, rolling over Ren's groggy mind.

"He wasn't exactly young," she mumbled.

"What?"

As out of it as she was, she still didn't want to sound stupid. She searched her sleepy brain for something smart. "But no one makes mummies anymore," she managed. She could still picture the Stung Man rising from his ancient sarcophagus, and later, once he'd replaced his wrappings with robes.

Alex just shrugged. "People aren't supposed to be filling English crypts with provisions for the afterlife, either," he said. "That must've been what he was there for: going back for seconds."

But then something did occur to Ren, something smart. She pictured the hand in the newspaper photo, covered in fresh linen. "If this Walker was newer, maybe they . . . I mean, maybe someone is still . . . like . . ." She paused to piece the thought together, but Alex had run out of patience.

"Where *is* she?" he blurted, turning to scan the road again.

Ren exhaled loudly. She was annoyed at being cut off, but it was more than that. She still felt so tired. It wasn't that she hadn't gotten enough sleep. She'd basically passed out as soon as she hit the bed. It was something else. She felt beaten up, hollowed out.

"I think I —" she began, but once again, Alex cut her off.

"We're wasting time," he said. There was no question who would keep talking, so Ren let him. "We'll just do it on our own until we hear from her."

"Yeah, 'cause that worked so well yesterday," she said.

Alex rolled on. "She's mad at us. She's probably out searching right now."

Ren doubted that. "She'll call soon," she said. "She left, like, a million messages yesterday. We just have to wait."

"We've *waited* too much already!" Alex sputtered, a fleck of saliva making it all the way to Ren's cheek. "What we need now is information. We need to find out who was in that tomb, for one. Really old info — the kind of stuff that won't be online. We need, like, a big library. Is there one in —"

"The British Library is one of the biggest in the world, Alex. How do you not know that?"

Finally, he looked over. Really looked. "What's your problem, Ren?" he said.

"What's *my* problem?" she said. "Where do I start? Did you even see what happened to us yesterday? What that thing did?"

"I saved you!" he protested.

"Saved me? You *dragged* me there — you served me up!"

"I was looking for *information*," he said. "I thought *you* could appreciate that."

Ren felt the dam burst within her. "Yeah, well, we got plenty of that. And we were free. Gone. We were on the path, headed down, and you had to STOP! Why? So stupid! '*Where's my mom?*'" She imitated his voice, made it whiny. "Really? You couldn't understand that thing if it told you!"

For a moment, she saw the words hit home. Then his eyes narrowed into slits. "I'm sorry if I'm not afraid to take chances," he spat. "*I* don't need to be perfect all the time. *I* don't need to know all the answers first."

"What do you —" she began, but she knew what he meant. Boy, did she.

Alex smirked, as if he'd proven something, as if he'd won. "We need to get going," he said firmly.

"We need to wait for Dr. Aditi!" said Ren. Now she was the one shouting. "Because *your* 'chances' are going to get *us* killed. And you know what *I* need?" She looked up at the sunny sky, the first really nice day since they'd arrived. "I need a break! From you, from this, from everything. I am tired, Alex . . . No," she corrected herself. "I am *drained*."

Alex stared at her, bug-eyed. "What do you want to —"

"I am going to go see the Rembrandts in the National Gallery. I've always wanted to do that."

Rembrandt was Ren's favorite painter, an Old Master of dark, lush portraits.

"But you can see those at the Met," said Alex.

"No! I can't! Because I am not *in* New York anymore, Alex. I'm in London! To help you, not that you've noticed."

Alex looked away. "You're homesick," he said. "You're scared."

The disappointment in his voice stung Ren, and for just a brief, dark moment, she dug down deep in her mind, looking for something sharp to wound him with. *At least I have parents at home to miss* flashed up like a monster from the deep, but she didn't say it. She took a deep breath.

"I am going to the National Gallery to look at the paintings and wait for Dr. Aditi to call," she said. She started down the sidewalk, pulling her guidebook from her messenger bag. "Have fun at the library."

Library Leads

Fine, thought Alex. *Fine.*

They could leave him alone, completely abandon him, if they wanted. Ren could go to a freaking gallery; Aditi could cut him out of her search. He'd done this before. He remembered the long spring days after he'd been pulled out of school. Sitting in his mom's office while she worked and Ren was in school, picking at his homeschool work like eating cold oatmeal. And he remembered the days in the hospital before that, waiting for his mom. Or anyone. So many days alone, and always waiting for someone.

Not anymore, he told himself. Now it was his mom who was alone. Now *she* was waiting for *him* — at least he hoped and prayed that she was. He felt sure that she was alive. *But how do I know? What if*... Alex shook his head *hard*, and his fast walk turned into almost a jog.

Soon, the massive British Library loomed before him. He was stunned by its size, and a jolt of hope shot through him.

Maybe the answers he needed were in there . . . He needed information on Egyptian Avenue. That seemed like a good place to start, but he knew what he was really looking for were potential Death Walkers: bad British dudes with some strong connection to Egypt . . .

Inside, the building was cool and clean and absolutely massive. Alex took a quick breath and got to it. It reminded him of the days he used to tag along with his mom to the main branch of the New York Public Library. This one was much larger and infinitely more British, but it contained the same mix of serious scholars, stressed students, gawking tourists, and the occasional crazy. Some books he could pluck from the shelves himself, and some he had to ask for.

An hour later, he was seated in a reading room on the third floor, in between the maps collection and Asian and African Studies. He had a heavy stack of old books on his desk and a thin layer of sweat on his forehead. He began with Highgate. He needed to figure out who was in that tomb: why the Walker had robbed it in the first place, and why he'd go back. His eyes glazed like doughnuts as he hit plenty of history in two newer books, but no mention of an unmarked vault. He skeptically picked up a very old, wafer-thin volume called *A Stroll Down Egyptian Avenue*.

The detailed description of the place sent a shiver through Alex. He remembered walking that same shadowy path — and what had waited at the end. And then: "As I walked on,

I came upon the unnamed vault and spared a thought for the notorious archaeologist within . . ." Alex held his breath, but the book's author spared only a thought, not a name.

An archaeologist, thought Alex. He glanced at the heavy stack of books in front of him, sighed, and went to get a whole new stack. He knew more or less what he was looking for: a "notorious" British archaeologist who'd died between 1839, when Highgate opened, and 1904, when the old book was written. He still wished his mom was there to ask all the right questions at the information desk. *My mom*, he thought, *or Ren*.

A Brush with Danger

Ren's head swam as she took a seat in front of a large painting, the old canvas thick and dark with layers of oil paint. Though she'd never seen it before, the painting was immediately familiar to her. It was by Rembrandt van Rijn, the Dutch painter whose work filled her favorite room back home at the Met. She followed the patterns in the paint slowly, allowing the faces and shapes they formed to come to her as if emerging from a lake.

She felt a knot loosen somewhere inside her. She could almost imagine she was back at the Met, waiting for her dad to finish work. Almost. But other images shouldered their way in. She reached a dark corner of the canvas, and instead of seeing the shadows of a long-ago room, she spied the open mouth of a monster. She shivered deep down but didn't look away.

She felt like she saw the impossible almost every day now. On a good day, it was a dead cat trying to get free. On a bad day, it was a dead man trying to suck out her soul . . . She felt like a visitor in her own world. Her facts, her lists: What good did they do when anything could be true? She pushed on, out of the corner of the canvas and back up. She found a face, the little brush of color on the cheek, and ever so slightly, she smiled.

And that's when she understood why she was there, in that room, instead of at the British Library. Yes, Alex was being selfish, but that wasn't it. She really was drained, and it wasn't her body that needed recharging. It wasn't her brain, either. She pulled her gaze back and took in the whole painting at once. It was beautiful.

No, it was her soul. She didn't understand how that was possible, either, but she knew this: It had nearly been torn from her, and now it needed to heal.

"Hey, Ren," she heard as someone sat down next to her.

She turned. "Oh, hey, Luke," she said, not quite managing to keep the surprise out of her voice.

"Hey," he said. "S'up?"

"Uh, not much?" said Ren. "Just checking out the paintings."

"Right, right," said Luke. "'Cause it's a gallery. Me too."

Ren didn't want to be rude, but . . . "Really?" she said. Luke was dressed as if a basketball game might break out at any moment. "Doesn't, uh, doesn't really seem like your thing."

"Oh, it's not, but the camp makes us," he said. "We have to 'tackle' cultural tasks. It's supposed to increase our mental sharpness or something. I'd like to tackle whoever came up with the idea before I die of boredom."

"Right," said Ren, picturing a small army of young jocks in knee-length shorts snickering at naked sculptures.

"Who painted this thing?" said Luke, nodding at the Rembrandt.

"You're kidding, right?"

The look on his face, as blank as the day is long, told her he wasn't. She sighed. "It's a Rembrandt."

Luke unfolded a piece of paper and took a small pen from his shorts. He scanned the paper but put the pen away without making a mark. "Oh, man," he said. "Already have that one."

"Bummer," said Ren, immediately regretting her sarcasm. Luke had saved her at the airport.

"Yeah," said Luke ruefully. "Say, where's A-Dawg at? Little twerp's not answering my messages."

"His battery died," she said, which was true enough.

Luke nodded. "So where's he at?"

Ren considered the question — and how much she should tell Luke. "Reading," she said. That also seemed true enough.

Luke looked at her carefully. *Does he know I'm ducking the question?* Most of the time she thought Luke was as dumb as a rock, but sometimes she wasn't so sure . . . "Like for his 'internship'?" he said.

The way he said it didn't ease her suspicions, but a moment later he was standing up and heading out of the room. "There are more of these Rembrandts two floors down."

"Thanks," she said, taking one last look and standing up herself.

"Tell my cuz to call me, okay?" said Luke. "Laterz!"

"Bye," said Ren, but he was already gone. He had paintings to cross off his list.

Ren checked her map. "Two floors down" . . . There was a level "–2" in the Sainsbury Wing — and it had "temporary exhibits." *That must be it*, she thought.

She reached the bottom of the stairs and found a guard. "Excuse me," she said, "I'm looking for the Rembrandts?"

"Ah, right, the special exhibit," he said. "Far corner, last room."

He pointed the way. She thanked him and walked on, a spring in her step for the first time in dog years.

She walked directly to the far corner, last room. Looking straight ahead, she didn't notice that the guard from the stairs was following her.

She entered the room like a summer breeze, light and warm. She looked around. She was the only one there, no people and no Rembrandts. These paintings were much earlier and entirely too English. She checked her map. The glass door swung shut behind her.

"'Ello again," she heard.

The summer breeze turned to an arctic chill. She'd been

so careful. Staying out of sight, blending in on the city's crowded sidewalks. But in this museum, feeling better for just a moment, she'd let her guard down. And now, she would pay for it.

She looked up and saw the thug from the airport: Liam, the van man. Behind him, through the closed glass door, she saw the guard from the stairs, taking up a post outside the room. *So stupid*, she thought.

"What do you want?" she said, stalling for time as her hand found her pocket.

"Nuffin' really," said Liam, a wicked grin lifting his thick lips. "No fuss. Jus' come wiv us."

Us? thought Ren. *How many of them are there?*

She ripped her phone free as she turned and ran. There was nowhere to go, no other exit, but she put the room's one bench in between her and the towering thug. As she shifted her weight from left to right, trying to guess which side he'd attack from, her shaking fingers fumbled across the screen. She managed to open her text messages. Liam had taken something from his pocket, too: a syringe.

Horse tranquilizer. It had nearly killed a guard twice her size. Liam took two quick steps and lunged. He stabbed out with the syringe as she punched her finger at the edge of the screen: *Send!* No bars down here. But maybe it would still —

"Aaaah!" she screamed as the point of the needle raked across her left arm. A long, deep scratch — but had any of

110

the tranquilizer gotten in? She ran around the right of the bench as Liam ran around the left. He was still behind it as she shot back across the room toward the door.

"Stop 'er!" he roared.

The guard turned around in time to see Ren throwing her whole body, messenger bag first, into the door. The thick safety glass smacked him in the face, and she squeezed out the small gap as Liam thundered up behind her.

The next room was empty, too, but she could see the exit at the far end. Desperate for escape, pulse pounding in her ears, she ran. Two steps, three — and she was yanked back. The guard had recovered in time to grab the strap of her messenger bag. He reeled her in like a wriggling trout as the drop of tranquilizer began to take effect and her vision began to blur.

Dark Discoveries

Alex was in a small basement reading room at the tail end of a search for one thick out-of-print book. He opened *Major British Archaeologists of the Nineteenth Century* and flipped to the index at the back. *First things first,* he thought. *What made an archaeologist notorious in the nineteenth century?*

He knew the answer immediately: It was a touchy subject in the museum world. He flipped to the *T*'s: "tomb raiding." Early on, he knew, it had been a free-for-all, with European powers openly plundering Egyptian tombs. Even Napoleon had gotten into the act. But this book covered a time that included the first rules, too, the first laws and restrictions. He scanned down the long list of page numbers for tomb raiding . . . Clearly not everyone was following the rules.

As he eyeballed the entries and wondered where to start, something occurred to him. Not even a thought yet, just an itch in his brain, a feeling that he was missing something. His mind flashed back to Highgate: the broken lid of the grave, the broken door of the crypt. *Robbed*, he thought. *Raided*.

The thought took shape: Was he on the trail of the crypt owner, or the Death Walker? He remembered his original goal: *a bad British dude with a strong connection to Egypt* . . . Sounded a lot like a notorious archaeologist to him.

He flipped to the *M*'s. There were dozens of entries for "mummies" . . . But only one for "mummified." It took him to Chapter 17, devoted entirely to one man:

"Discharged from the military for his habit of torturing prisoners, Captain Winfred Willoughby began a second career. He called himself a 'gentleman archaeologist' but was, by all accounts, a professional tomb raider. This too ended when he fled Egypt while awaiting trial for multiple counts of theft and the murder of a rival archaeologist and two young diggers . . ."

Yeah, thought Alex, *that's a bad British dude, all right.*

He skipped down the page:

"Seeking to ensure his own 'immortality,' Willoughby set aside a large sum in his will to have his body mummified. With no experienced practitioners available, however, the procedure was botched. According to contemporary accounts, the ceremonial washing was skipped, and while the other five steps were attempted" — Alex ran through them in his head: removing the organs, drying the body with salts, packing it with more salts, sealing it with resin, and wrapping it all up — "the hired help barely knew which end to hold the de-braining hook by . . ."

Alex paused to turn the page, his head abuzz: a botched mummy, a mummy made by amateurs . . . He remembered the Walker's ravaged voice and mottled skin. He read the last few lines:

"The mummification was such a scandal at the time that the cemetery where he was interred refused to list Willoughby's name on his crypt."

A crude early photo filled the rest of the page, blurry black-and-white. The subject looked smaller and less impressive than the figure they'd encountered at Highgate. His shoulders were slighter, his chest less broad, but the face and even the outfit left no doubt.

No one broke into that mausoleum.

Willoughby broke out.

Alex snapped the book shut, and two names floated through his thunderstruck mind: that of his new enemy and that of his best friend.

I've got to tell Ren, he thought as he took the stairs two at a time. He was eager to see the sun after his dark discoveries, and ready to make amends. He pictured her face lighting up as he relayed the info.

Midway up the stairs, reception returned and his phone began buzzing with missed messages. *Aditi*, he thought. *Now I'm going to get it.* He glanced down at the screen as he reached the top of the stairs. He was half-right: Someone was in trouble. He nearly ran face-first into the door as he read Ren's message:

bAsement nat gallery cornerd VAN MAN1 HELP

His heart sank as his pulse soared. He raced toward the exit. He wasn't even going to read the second text — the latest from Luke — but the first line was already visible on the screen:

Just saw R at galory. Where u at playa . . .

Alex swiped back to Ren's message and nearly put his finger through the screen as he punched her name to call her. He went through the front door of the library as his call went to voice mail.

He asked the first three people he saw how to get to the National Gallery. The third guy knew: He had to take the Northern Line again, heading south this time. Alex burned with impatience as he listened. Van Man — Liam — could already have her. He wished he was there already, and suddenly he realized he knew someone who was. *"Saw R at galory."*

As he sprinted across the street toward Euston station, he punched his phone again. The time had come to return his cousin's messages. The Order had its muscle. The friends needed some of their own.

It was a quick, urgent phone call. With someone else, Alex might have had to convince him that the danger was real. But Luke had already seen Liam in action. His last words before Alex lost signal in the station: "I'm on it!"

The train took minutes but felt like hours. When it finally pulled into Charing Cross, Alex burst through the door and broke free ahead of the pack like a racehorse. He dodged fast cars and slow walkers and flew into the grand old building that housed the National Gallery. The first guards protested his pace — "Slow down there!" — but it wasn't until the fourth guard that he ran into real trouble. The man was standing at the top of the stairwell, and Alex recognized his face from the airport.

Alex grasped his amulet as they raced toward each other. Half a dozen museumgoers turned to watch. From their vantage point behind the action, it looked like the boy had pushed the guard with incredible force, sending him tumbling down the stairs. Only the "guard" had a clear view of what had really happened. The force had come from the boy's hand, all right, but he had never touched him.

Alex charged down the stairs, hopping over the tumbling thug and leaving him lying on the landing. But when he reached the bottom of the stairs, he found himself in a battleground. Ren was lying on the floor, eyes closed and hands tied. Liam was kneeling next to her, wearing her messenger bag over his shoulder and wrapping her bound wrists with a scarf. Luke was backed into a corner facing two more thugs, one wearing a guard's uniform.

"'Bout time, cuz!" Luke called. He was standing in a wide stance with his arms out and his palms up, like an NFL lineman. He was cornered, but neither of the thugs seemed too eager to rush in on him. Alex could only imagine the tackles and turns his cousin had used to stall them so far.

Liam followed Luke's eyes and spun around. He didn't seem particularly surprised to see Alex. "Look 'ooz 'ere!" bellowed the big man.

Alex gritted his teeth and squeezed down hard on his amulet. *The wind that comes before the rain,* he thought as he raised his free hand. He squeezed his fingers into a sharp point and corrected himself. *The wind that comes before the* pain.

A lance of concentrated air caught Liam directly under his chin, sending him reeling backward. As the other thugs turned and shifted to get out of the way, Luke Quicksilvered out between them. Without slowing down, he lowered his shoulder and crashed into the back of Liam's legs, sending the big man toppling over him and onto the floor.

"How'd you do that?" said Luke, a look of sheer bafflement on his flushed face. "It looked like you just, like, pointed at him."

Alex glanced down at the scarab. *I'll have to tell him*, he thought. But it would have to wait. "Behind you!" called Alex.

The other thugs were scrambling over their lardy leader as Liam rubbed his head and tried to right himself. Luke darted to the right and then quickly cut back to the left, leaving the closest bruiser grasping at air.

The thugs switched targets and rushed toward Alex. He couldn't knock them both down at once with his wind power. His eyes sought out the biggest, heaviest object in the room. Unfortunately for Liam, that was him. Alex didn't know if he could hoist that much weight, but as the thugs raced toward him, they also raced toward Ren. She was defenseless on the floor, and the thought that they would kick into her filled him with rage — and power.

As Liam rose onto one knee, his body jerked violently off the floor and spun toward the other two men. His big frame caught them at shoulder level and all three landed in a heap on the cold tile floor, grunting from pain and surprise.

"All right, seriously, what was that?" said Luke, rushing up to join Alex. "There's no way that big dude could jump like that."

They both instinctively took up a defensive position over Ren's limp body.

"Get the one wiv da trinket!" shouted Liam, climbing back to his feet. "'E's the one we really want. Cut 'is bleedin' 'ands off if ya need to!"

Alex heard a pair of mechanical *shnikks* as the two thugs rose from the floor with switchblades in their hands. The sharp steel caught the white museum light.

Seven or eight museumgoers had come down the stairs to see what all the shouting was about. "They've got knives!" one of them shouted, and a real museum guard came running up.

Liam surveyed the growing crowd with a snarl of disdain. He glanced down at Ren. Alex caught his gaze and gave him a look of his own: *Don't even think about it.*

"You ain't seen the last of us, boys!" called Liam.

The thugs bolted toward the stairs. The tourists shrieked and parted to let the knife-wielding goons pass. The lone guard made a valiant attempt at doing his duty, but Liam dismissed him with one powerful punch to the gut.

"My bag . . ."

The voice was weak but welcome. Ren was awake. She raised her head off the floor and squinted up toward the stairs as her would-be kidnappers disappeared from view. By the time Alex could take hold of his amulet again, the familiar olive green messenger bag had already been carried off on Liam's shoulder.

"Sorry," Alex said, looking down at his bleary-eyed friend. "I am so, so sorry."

They both knew he wasn't just talking about the bag.

Aftermath

They were a strange sight, the three of them. Alex walked on one side of Ren, bending down to support her. Luke walked on the other side, bending down even farther, since he was taller than both of them. Ren, for her part, had the look of a sleepwalker: her eyes just cracked open and her steps unsure.

From the steps of the gallery, a guard called out to them to come back and wait for the police, but he quickly lost sight of them in the shifting throng of the midday metropolis. Fellow pedestrians eyed them suspiciously. But soon they were back in the relative safety of the good old Northern Line. Once the train doors closed behind them, Ren became just another sleepy kid, jet-lagged perhaps.

Luke leaned across her to talk to Alex: "Why didn't we wait for the cops?"

Alex shushed him as a few nearby heads turned. Luke was surprised by the shushing, and Alex was stumped by the question. *How could he explain this to his cousin?* Where would he even start: the powerful death cult for whom the police were no obstacle, or the full story, ancient spells and all, that would land them all in a mental institution? He glanced down at the spot where his amulet rested beneath his shirt.

"What is that thing?" Luke whispered. "There's no way those guys were just throwing themselves around. You *did* that, right? With that bug thing?"

Alex gave Luke a look: *Not now!*

"Well, at least tell me where we're going," he said, leaning back.

"Servants' quarters," mumbled Ren from the seat between them.

The three shaken friends settled back — into their seats, and into their thoughts. Alex's were dark, as usual, but also unusually clear. His grim mood and obsessive behavior had driven his best friend away — and alone, she was easy prey. The thought that she could have suffered the same fate as his mom — kidnapped, taken from him — had rocked him to his core. As the train rumbled toward its destination, he stewed in a mix of guilt at himself, anger at The Order, and gratitude for Ren's safety — and Luke's help.

He glanced over at his cousin, who looked troubled, too. Luke caught his cousin's eyes and whispered one last word to him, very clearly: "Knives." Alex nodded, but Luke had already looked away. Once again, he had taken running into the thugs in stride — literally — but the fact that they were armed this time had clearly caught him off guard. Luke wasn't used to the rules changing mid-game.

Ren sat silently, sleepily between them. If she was still angry at Alex, she didn't show it. In fact, as the train jounced and jostled along, he felt her lean against him for support. The needle-torn sleeve of her injured shoulder felt rough against his arm. He understood her instinctively, the way that best friends do sometimes: *We're both hurting. It's okay.*

The train reached their stop, and the three disembarked. Enveloped by the anonymous chatter of the crowd, they could speak more freely now. And Luke had something to say. "I don't know what you two are up to," he announced, "but it's more exciting than this camp. And no one at the camp has tried to stab me, either. I want payback. I want *in.*"

Alex and Ren exchanged quick glances. No need for discussion. Luke wanted in? After what he'd just seen? After saving their bacon for a second time? They just nodded. He was in already.

On the way back they stopped at a Tesco — a British chain that fell somewhere between supermarket and 7-Eleven — and loaded up on food and snacks. Mostly snacks. Then they walked into the little parking lot of the Campbell Collection.

"Home again, home again," said Alex.

Ren removed a Cadbury chocolate bar from the plastic bag, the last wisps of fog lifting from her eyes. "Jiggety-jog," she answered.

On the other end of town, Liam was about to learn that when you work for a death cult, failure has its consequences.

"Where ya takin' me, then?" he asked, nervously eyeing the dark tunnel walls around him. Cut at a steep downward angle, the dirt and rock and clay didn't feel very secure. *He* wasn't feeling very secure, either.

Still no answer from his guide. He risked a quick glance over, but the man's expression was hidden under a heavy iron mask in the shape of a crocodile head, like a knight's visored helmet gone wild.

"What's your name again?" he asked nervously. He knew the man beneath the mask was powerful and dangerous, but the subterranean silence was driving him batty. He wanted to hear a voice other than his own.

"Ta-mesah." The word came out in a low, reptilian hiss that sent a chill through Liam's system.

"Tommy what?" he said.

The other man looked over at him, leveling the sinister snout of the mask in his direction. Liam could just make out two small, dark eyes. "Ta-MESAH!" the man repeated.

Liam still didn't understand but nodded anyway.

The tunnel led steadily down into the dark English dirt. Liam looked up at the roof of the tunnel, where an uneven stripe down the center gave off a greenish-white glow, providing the only light. *Must be one of those funguses*, he thought.

The kind what glow in the dark. He'd seen something about them on the BBC.

More nervous the deeper they went, Liam continued his questions. "Where ya takin' me?"

Ta-mesah was silent for a few more steps and then: "There's someone I'd like you to meet."

Liam wondered who on earth that might be. He'd already been told — they all had — that the man in the mask was in charge. The tunnel opened up into a larger chamber, and Ta-mesah slowed down half a step to allow him to enter first. Liam stepped inside.

A very large man stood behind a stone slab near the back of the room, regarding Liam with black, lightless eyes.

Liam felt a gut-punch of fear and confusion at the sight, but he did his best to collect himself. "You, uh, wanted ta see me?"

The looming figure croaked out a ragged response. Liam didn't understand a word of it, but his masked guide seemed to.

"Another minion for you," said Ta-mesah.

Minion? thought Liam.

The sleeve of the man's filthy shirt was rolled up, and he was pushing through an array of sharp metal tools on a tray in front of him. The implements clinked against each other as Willoughby made his selection. He raised a thin bronze probe, as long as a forearm and tipped with a small, sharp hook. Unlike the clods who'd prepared him, Willoughby knew which end to hold the thing by. He looked at Liam . . . and smiled.

"Right, then," said Liam, more to himself than to the two men he was now sure meant to kill him. He'd been a loyal employee, if not an especially effective one, and The Order had paid him well. But there comes a point when even a company man needs to declare free agency.

He turned quickly on the heel of his boot — always fast for his size — and made for the tunnel.

Ta-mesah casually raised his right hand from beneath his long dark robe and brought it back down — just a quick flick of the wrist.

At the mouth of the tunnel, Liam felt his body lift off the ground, his feet kicking out from underneath him. He could only flap his arms helplessly as he was slammed back down. The back of his head crashed into the hard-packed dirt and knocked him out cold.

A small boy wearing clothes nearly as dirty as his master's emerged from the tunnel.

"Why is the little one alive?" said Ta-mesah as he stepped aside to let the child pass.

Willoughby put down the hook and waggled his thick, sausage-like fingers. Ta-mesah understood: Mummification was an intricate process. It required nimble fingers.

A crude figure shambled in after the boy and began dragging Liam's limp body toward the stone slab. The creature stooped and pulled against the big man's weight, its fresh, tight wrappings straining and fraying from the effort. A second figure joined it, and together they lifted the body onto the cold stone slab.

Ta-mesah assessed the creatures' decidedly non-nimble movements. *They lose something after death*, he thought.

The boy took up his post — his eyes haunted, his movements mechanical — and handed Willoughby his hook.

Far overhead, back above the surface and another few thousand feet up besides, strange clouds grew thicker and began to turn as Willoughby moved on to the next steps. The sky above opened up.

Ta-mesah watched the mummification with a detached, vaguely academic interest. He'd already known what had become of London's missing. Now, as the scent of the red rain filtered down into the murky air of the tomb, he understood what triggered that, too. He was more familiar than most with the ancient proverb: blood for blood.

It meant little to him. He'd been sent here to aid the Walker, and he had done so. But he had no doubt who he was really serving.

Let the Englishman have his crude toys, he thought. *Soon we will have true immortality, and the power that comes with it.*

Breaking News

The three friends were huddled together in Alex's room. They were staring at the headline on the screen of Ren's laptop: "The Dr Is Out."

Aditi was gone. Alex scanned the story quickly. "Last seen leaving the British Museum after a day of emergency meetings . . . Observed talking on a cell phone, the records to which have not been recovered."

He knew why. It was disposable. Todtman had used one in New York, too, to keep their secret mission off his own phone.

"Was she talking?" he said, thinking out loud. "Or leaving us messages?"

Alex looked back at the screen, at the picture of Aditi, smiling just slightly beneath the tacky tabloid headline. All this time he'd thought they were in trouble, when really it was her. He remembered the argument in her office, how his impatience had brought out the worst in him again. More guilt, more fuel for his dark fire.

"Do you think, like, this cult got her?" said Luke. "'The Order,'" he added, making the air quotes with his fingers.

"I almost hope so," said Alex. Because there was another possibility, one they hadn't told Luke about yet. He remembered the gray shadow slipping from his body, the open mouth of the Walker.

"I can't look at this anymore," said Ren, getting to her feet.

Alex looked at her: *Was she remembering the same thing, seeing her own soul torn from its moorings? Or, adrenaline used up, had the tranquilizer finally caught up with her?* He tried to make eye contact with her, to get an idea of what she was thinking, but she was already heading toward the door.

"You can keep my computer for now," she said as she exited.

Alex watched his door close and a moment later heard her door open. He turned back to find his cousin looking directly at him.

"All right, cuz," said Luke, "I'm not as smart as you, and I'm definitely not as smart as her, but I'm smart enough to know there's something you two aren't telling me."

Alex nodded. He'd already decided to let Luke know what was going on and had barely bothered to hide it when he'd pulled Ren aside to tell her about Willoughby. There'd be no more keeping Luke in the dark — he'd seen so much already.

Alex took a deep breath. "Some of this is going to sound pretty crazy, and it might be kind of hard to believe," he began. He carefully pulled the amulet from under his shirt and closed his left hand around it. "So first I want you to watch something."

And there, in the tiny room, Alex put on a little show. It was nothing much. He was still nursing a headache from the fight. He stacked some books, closed the window, flicked the light on and off, all with the wave of a hand. When he was done, Luke's eyes were wide with wonder.

Alex told him everything. Well, almost everything. For some reason, he couldn't bring himself to tell his cousin how it had all started: with him lying on life support and his mom unfurling the Lost Spells in his hospital room. He couldn't bring himself to admit that one simple fact: that all of this — everything that had happened in New York and London and Cairo and around the world — was because of him.

When he was done, Luke looked down at the floor and then back at the story still filling the laptop screen. Finally, he looked at his cousin. "So," he began, and Alex could see his cousin struggling to comprehend the incomprehensible. "That's not algae out there, then, is it?"

Luke nodded toward the window. The rain had started again. The glass had turned red.

"So what do we do?" said Luke.

Alex peeled his eyes from the window and looked at his cousin.

"Remember that place I just told you about, Highgate?" said Alex. "We're gonna have to go back there."

"We have to go to a cemetery?" said Luke.

Alex pictured the Walker's mud-streaked clothing. "Under one," he said.

Alex knew he should probably be doing more research, but as the rain poured down, and as Ren rested next door, he spent the afternoon asking Luke everything he remembered about his aunt Maggie. They were simple memories — after-hours tours of the museum, the bike she bought him for his seventh birthday — but they meant the world to Alex. Right now, memories were all he had left of his mom.

Burning Daylight

Finally, Alex knew he needed to snap back into action. He headed down the creaky stairs, Luke close behind him.

It was just after five and the museum was already closed when they reached the first floor. Somers was puttering around, flicking off lights and straightening up. One look at him told them that he was upset. Eyes heavy and face puffy, it looked like he might even have been crying. Alex thought he knew why.

"You and Dr. Aditi are close, right?"

Somers stopped what he was doing and turned toward him. "She . . . Priya . . . she was like a daughter to me," he said. "I was her professor once. In another life, feels like."

The word *was* echoed in Alex's head. *Was* like a daughter . . . And he wasn't the only one to hear it.

"We could still find her."

It was Ren, appearing at the edge of the room. Her hair was rumpled from sleep but her eyes were alert. Somers gave her a tired smile, and a wave of guilt washed over Alex when he saw it. He felt responsible for all of the disappearances — so many had suffered because he'd been saved — but for this one especially.

"What do you need from me?" asked Somers. "I take it this isn't a social call."

"The Book of the Dead," Alex said without hesitation. "We were going to get it from the British Museum, once we figured out which spell . . ."

His voice trailed off. He hadn't exactly done that yet, but he had a good idea of the type of spell he needed. He thought he'd know it when he saw it . . .

"Why do we need a book?" said Luke, who had never had much use for them.

But this part Alex *was* sure of. "This is a battle now," he said. "They got Dr. Aditi, and they almost got Ren. We need to get them. We need to stop Willoughby, the Death Walker. He's why all this is happening, just like in New York."

He searched his brain for the right expression and found it: "We need to cut off the head of the snake."

"You can do that with the Book, can't you?" said Somers. "You can send 'im back."

Alex looked at Somers and nodded. Aditi had said they could trust him, but now he found himself wondering how much did the old man — the old professor — already know. How much she had told him.

"Can we still get it?" he said. "The Book of the Dead, I mean. Can you get it?"

Another tired smile. "What, the old caretaker from the Campbell is going to waltz into the British Museum and walk out with an armful of ancient texts?"

Alex considered it. The security at the British would be world-class, especially right now. Without Aditi, that would be another battle . . .

"But we do have some of the Book here," said Somers.

Alex shook his head. "I checked that out when we first got here," he said. "It's just a few spells from the beginning."

"But we know more now," said Ren. "You should check it again."

"But . . ." Alex said.

"We only need one," she said.

"I guess it's worth a shot," he admitted.

The case was a few rooms over. Alex surveyed the sparse selection of papyrus and linen, all covered with the rows of small symbols that made up hieroglyphic writing and illus-trated with little paintings. Gods and humans, judges and judged.

Alex wrapped his left hand around the scarab and felt the cold stone warm to his touch, as if alive. In the dim light of the closed collection, the ancient writing in front of him began to glow softly.

Alex's eyes scanned the battered pages. As the words became clear, he read the titles out loud. Not quite a dozen in total: "For Going Out into the Day" . . . "For Breathing in the Land of the Dead" . . . Finally, his hand fell from his amulet, the glow faded, and the white returned to his eyes.

"Not here," he said. "It's none of these."

The energy drained from the room like air from a week-old birthday balloon.

Suddenly, Alex turned to face Somers. "But there are more here, aren't there?"

"More?" said Somers.

"Yes, more of the Book, other spells," said Alex. "I could feel them."

Somers looked confused for a moment, but then his expression cleared. "You're right," he said. "In the basement. But they're in rough shape. Not suitable for display."

Alex smiled grimly. "We don't need to display them."

The basement was more shadow than light. Thick cobwebs in the corners and a shifting layer of dust on the floors completed the effect.

"Lovely," said Ren, hanging back a bit as Somers rummaged through rusty cabinets and crumpled boxes.

"Is that it?" said Alex. "That old box, under that table?"

Somers flipped the box around and blew some dust off. Three letters came into view, written in faded Magic Marker: B.O.D.

"It's either that or a body," he said wryly, lifting the box up and dropping it down with a dull thud on the table.

It was mostly scraps — the archaeological equivalent of a

junk drawer — but Alex went through it carefully. He had one hand on his amulet and one doing the sorting, and he knew immediately that these were better. The spells upstairs had been the general ones, from the beginning of the Book: the ones to help the soul first enter the afterlife. These were the specific ones, the nitty-gritty . . . He spread the spells that were still in good enough shape to read out on the table.

Once again, he reached for his amulet and the ancient text came alive as he read:

"For Causing a Man to Be a Spirit in the Land of the Dead."

"For Protection Against Snakes in the Land of the Dead."

"For Protection Against Grave Robbers and Outland Thieves."

"For Going Forth and Coming Back."

Alex stopped. Went back one: *For Protection Against Grave Robbers and Outland Thieves.* The glow faded from the hieroglyphs and his eyes refocused on the world around him. He held up the scraggly scrap of linen, a single patch of what had once been a mummy's wrappings.

"I think this is it," he said.

"That?" said Luke. "It looks like a three-thousand-year-old cafeteria napkin — from pizza day."

Alex smiled. The ancient Egyptians had contributed many things to civilization — advances in math and medicine, door locks, and even toothpaste — but pizza wasn't one of them. Somers opened a manila folder and Alex carefully deposited the spell inside.

"Are you sure?" said Ren.

Unlike Luke, she understood the stakes. A Death Walker could only be sent back to the afterlife with exactly the right spell. They'd brought three to their battle with the Stung Man. This time they'd be bringing one — or what was left of it.

"I'm sure," said Alex. But even as he said it he wondered: How much did he really know about Willoughby?

"If you're wrong . . ." said Ren.

She didn't need to finish the thought. Alex understood. *If I'm wrong*, he thought, *we're* dead *wrong*. He thought back to what he'd read: "a professional tomb raider . . . multiple counts of theft . . ." *It has to be*, he thought. *Doesn't it?*

"This is the one," he said, filling his voice with more confidence than he felt. He was ready for a rematch with the Walker, and this was his ticket. But he had one more concern as he closed the folder on the dry and fragile linen. "I just hope the thing doesn't fall apart on us."

They filed out of the grim basement.

"Need anything else?" said Somers, closing the door behind them.

They all considered the question.

"Got a shovel?" said Alex.

"And flashlights," said Ren.

Luke thought about it for another moment. "I could use a Gatorade," he said.

The Gathering Dark

They rode the train in silence, on their own again. Somers was back at the museum, "in reserve." He'd wanted to come along, but they'd insisted — and practically run out of the place ahead of him. He would only slow them down. At his age he had enough trouble walking, forget about running.

Luke tried to imagine that: a life without running. It was the scariest thing yet. But then he hadn't seen this "Death Walker" thingamajig the others kept talking about. That sounded pretty scary, too. The train bumped to a stop, and Alex's overstuffed backpack shifted and clanked on the floor.

"We're here," said Ren, not sounding too happy about it.

Luke stood up, grabbing Alex's backpack without asking. He was stronger, and besides, he wanted his cousin to have his hands free in case he had to use that magic bug of his. It seemed crazy, but after what he'd seen, he was willing to go with the flow on this magic stuff. There was lots of stuff he didn't understand. Like why could he already dunk at thirteen when most guys would never dunk in their life? He had a saying for things like that: *Don't break your brain.*

"Seems like a waste," said Ren as they waited for the elevator to the street.

Luke didn't get it until they were halfway up.

"Because we're going right back underground?" he said to Ren.

She nodded, but he could see she was a million miles away. He didn't understand her the way he did his cousin — he'd known his little cousin was up to something as soon as Alex moved into the spare room next to his. But this girl, with her mouth clamped shut and her eyes wide open? Was that fear? Determination? Both?

They left the station and headed up the hill toward the cemetery. The sky was getting dark now, laced with twilight purple. The hill was steep — good workout for the quadriceps — but halfway up, the other two stopped. Luke doubled back to see what the holdup was. In an ideal world, he'd like to reach the cemetery before it was full-on dark. Not that he was scared or anything . . .

Alex and Ren were talking to an older couple handing out flyers. "No luck so far," said the lady, "but if just one person remembers seeing him that night . . ."

Luke looked over at the flyer she was holding. He could just make out the photo in the dim light. His eyes immediately went to the trophy. *Third place*, he thought. *That's sad.* But it reminded him where he'd seen it before.

"You're looking for your nephew, right?" he said.

"Yes," said the man. "Our little Robbie."

"Right, right," said Luke. "Good luck."

They resumed their march up the hill. Luke's steps were heavier now, and it wasn't his quads. *Little kids*, he thought. *Was that The Order's doing, too, or was it this Death Walker? And, if what Alex said was true, was there even a difference?* One final thought formed in his head, clearer than the others, six simple words: *What have I signed up for?*

The streets of Highgate were empty now. The old couple were the last two people they saw. There was barely even any traffic, save for a few slowly cruising police cars.

"Through here," said Ren, pointing to a sign that read WATERLOW PARK.

The park was empty, the failing light robbing it of its color. The only sounds were night birds warming to their task; the only movement, a flock of geese drifting aimlessly across a dark pond. As they exited, Luke saw Highgate Cemetery looming like a city of the dead. At its base, across a narrow road, a single light burned.

They stepped away from the trees and crossed the road. A light London fog had formed on the mossy hillside, as it did most nights, making the ground above them appear lighter than the sky. At the main gate, the windows of the building next to it were dark. "We're alone," said Luke.

Alex reached up and clasped his amulet. "No, we're not."

Crypt

Alex used his amulet to force open the big lock on the main gate.

"First try, bro!" said Luke as the heavy tumbler turned.

Alex began to push the gate open.

"Wait," said Ren.

"What?" said Alex, spinning around. "Did you see something?"

"No, it's just . . . Do we have to do this right now? At night?"

"You're kidding me," said Alex. "We're already here!"

"Yeah, but I was thinking, we could go back, do some more research, make sure we have everything we need . . ."

"And come back in the morning!" added Luke.

Alex didn't bother to hide his annoyance. "Go home if you want to," he snapped. "I'm going in."

He pushed the gate the rest of the way open and slipped inside. The others exchanged quick glances but followed reluctantly. The soft soles of their sneakers padded silently across the stone courtyard, and soon they reached the stairway cut into the hill. Alex paused at the bottom to look at the layered shadows of trees and tombstones and crosses and crypts.

"Dark up there," said Luke.

"Really dark," said Ren. "Should we get the flashlights?"

Alex looked up. The moon was barely visible behind a shifting curtain of clouds. Still, they couldn't risk being seen. "No," said Alex. "If we stick to the main path, we'll be fine."

The pale stone of the stairs caught what little light there was. Alex took a deep breath and led the way. The others followed a few steps behind. The main trail was a little lighter, but not much. At first, Alex could follow it if he squinted. But as they climbed up the hill, the fog rolled down it. Soon their feet were enveloped in cottony mist. Along the sides, the crypts and tombstones erupted like dark islands out of the gray, framing the pathway.

"These tombstones are huge!" hissed Luke.

"That's 'cause the people are inside," Alex whispered back.

"WHAT?" said Luke, his voice rising.

He got shushed again and then Alex added: "They buried them aboveground."

Luke looked over at the nearest gravesite: a long stone rectangle covered in elaborate floral carvings. He gave it a wave and a whisper: "Hey, dude."

"Shhhh," hissed Ren. "We're almost there."

"Where?" whispered Luke.

Ren's glare was wasted in the dark.

Alex answered: "Egyptian Avenue."

The three gathered along one side of the archway at the entrance. They peered inside but couldn't see anything in the narrow lane between the crypts. Pitch-dark, dead quiet. They listened for a solid minute before they were ready.

"Flashlights," Alex whispered.

Luke swung the backpack off gracefully, without a single clunk or clang, and they all reached in and took one.

"Point 'em down," said Alex.

The flashlights lightsabered the fog at their feet.

Alex edged closer to Ren as they began a slow procession toward Willoughby's crypt. "You okay?" he whispered.

"Little late if I wasn't," she shot back.

Caught off guard, he didn't know how to respond. Should he apologize? "I . . . I'm . . ."

"I'm fine, Alex," she said, but a quiver in her voice said otherwise. Her next words were steadier: "I just want to get this over with."

"How will we know which one?" Luke hissed, shining his light on each heavy, black-painted door they passed. But the next door his light hit was leaning open. "Never mind," he whispered. "Found it."

Finding it was one thing. Going in was another. The three friends stood outside the door and looked at each other in the glow of the flashlights. Then, very slowly, Ren and Luke turned and looked at Alex.

"Yeah," he breathed, turning to face the door. "Okay."

His front foot was on the edge of the open doorway. He

142

brought his back foot up to join it. Standing on the line between life and death, he took one last look at his friends. He felt his pulse in his head and the cool night breeze against his cheek. He raised his flashlight and stepped forward . . .

Something lashed out and struck his cheek as he crossed the doorway.

Panic rose in his gut as whatever it was brushed against his face again. He whirled around, grabbing his amulet with one hand and pointing his flashlight with the other. It was . . .

"Just some old cloth," he heard Luke say.

Centered in the beam of his flashlight, Alex saw a six-inch strip of white fabric. It was caught on the ragged inside edge of the doorway and flapping lightly in the breeze.

Alex lowered his flashlight, released the scarab, and looked back at his friends. Luke was wearing a big smile and pointing at him: *busted!*

But Ren was looking him right in the eye, and Alex knew why. They'd both seen fresh linen like this before, or at least a picture of it.

"Come on, you guys," said Alex, waving them inside.

The crypt had a musty smell, and Alex washed his flashlight beam along the near wall, illuminating a full row of tall ceramic jars. He imagined the 170-year-old bread and dried beef and grains inside, glad the lids were still on.

"A statue!" called Ren, shining her light into the far corner.

"Whoa!" said Luke. "Look at that bad boy."

A stone statue of Captain Willoughby stood in one corner of the crypt, pointing at some imaginary discovery in the distance. Alex waved his flashlight over the looming figure. "It looks just like him," he said, and it did: Same face, same outfit, same size. "*Just* like him."

He fixed his light on the statue's eyes. They were just as blank as he remembered, but instead of pure black, they were the elegant off-white of marble. Alex held the beam there for an extra second, just to make sure the eyes didn't blink. He exhaled. "It's weird," he said, remembering the old photo. "This dude was a lot dumpier in real life."

"Here's his stone box thing," said Luke. "He was buried aboveground, too."

Key word: *was.* The lid was off and Alex knew the lead inner coffin would be empty, too, before he even dipped his flashlight beam inside. If the Walker were here, he would've felt it.

A question formed in the darkness: *So where is he? And what about the mummy that left that scrap of wrapping?*

Alex looked back at the doorway, the wisp of cloth still flapping lightly in the breeze. *The breeze.* He licked his finger and held it up. The breeze was shifting back and forth, coming from the back of the chamber as much as the door. He stepped slowly around the old stone coffin toward the back wall.

"Shovel," he said, holding out his hand.

"Shovel," said Luke, reaching into the pack and handing over an old folding shovel from Somers's army days.

They'd reached the crypt. Now they had to go deeper.

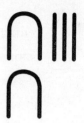

Down, Down, Down

They used the little collapsible shovel not to dig but to pry. Ren shot one more quick, nervous look behind her as Alex folded the blade halfway out and locked it into place. He slid it under the edge of the large stone slab they'd discovered against the back wall and leaned in with all his weight. Nothing. He bounced against the handle, grunted, strained. Nothing. He handed the shovel back to Luke, who was already stepping forward to take it.

Luke didn't bounce or strain, just leaned in and applied slow, steady pressure. Ren watched him work, and the confident way he moved eased her ragged nerves a little. He had an undeniable sense for anything physical. Sure enough, the stone began to slide to the side. Once there was enough of a gap, the three of them got together and pushed.

A faint glow spilled out as the gap widened. Ren let the boys finish up as she gazed inside. It was a tunnel sloping down into the hillside, with an eerie glow coming from the ceiling. She swallowed hard. She'd seen this sort of thing before: in the Stung Man's tomb.

Alex took his pack back — because it held the spell — and Ren grabbed the little shovel to use as a weapon.

"Flashlights off," said Alex, standing in the eerie green-white light.

Ren looked at the back of his head as she dropped her light in the backpack. He was getting bossy again. With every bad thing that had happened to them, he'd grown angrier and more determined. He'd been halfway decent to her for what, half a day after the attack? And now he was leading them down this dark, dirty tunnel. He was rushing them. *Why not take another night? Let me see that archaeologist book for myself? And maybe a few more?* She felt unprepared, and she *hated* that.

To try to calm herself down, she made a mental list of all the reasons she had for being there: (1) for Alex, who needed her, (2) for his mom, who was almost like family to her, too, (3) for Aditi, (4) for that poor missing kid, and all the other ones, too, (5) AGAINST that monster, (6) AGAINST The Order . . .

They moved cautiously down the tunnel, feet slow, eyes wide. Ren turned her head slightly to put one ear forward, listening for the faintest sound.

Ten feet ahead, there was an opening. Flickering candle-light spilled out from inside. They crept up to it and stopped

146

just short. Alex grasped his amulet tighter and Ren raised her shovel. They nodded at each other. Alex ducked his head inside.

He was silent for a few long seconds. Ren held her breath. *Had he seen something horrible? Something they hadn't even thought to fear?*

He raised his hand and waved them in. She exhaled. "All clear," he whispered.

It was a little side room, the last stop on the way out of the tomb or the first stop on the way in, like the mudroom in a house. Ren looked around: It was a pretty fancy mudroom. The walls, and even the ceiling, had been covered with a smooth plaster. Silver sconces held thick wax candles, and on a little shelf in the center of one wall was the single shiniest thing Ren had ever seen.

"Wow," said Luke.

"Is that . . . ?" said Alex.

"One of the Crown Jewels," said Ren. It was a golden orb ringed and topped with a galaxy of glittering gems. She'd seen it while poring over her guidebook: *the Sovereign's Orb, maybe?* It reminded her of the stolen finery in the Stung Man's inner sanctum, but only a little. "The last one just had some, like, really nice rugs," she said.

"This one is more powerful," said Alex, already turning away from the world-famous relic. "He's been awake longer."

Ren had seen Willoughby's power for herself, of course, but a new thought rocked her now: *How powerful could these things get?*

"Let's go," said Alex.

They followed him back out into the hallway. Ren knew why he was so angry and driven, and she really hoped he found his mom soon.

1) Because she was worried about her, too.

2) Because she was worried about what the search was doing to him.

3) Because she was pretty sure he'd get them all killed if he didn't find her soon.

Back out in the hallway, disaster struck almost immediately.

Something's coming.

Alex stopped and put his right hand up.

"What?" said Ren.

"Something's coming," he said.

"I didn't hear anything," she whispered.

He shook his head. It wasn't something he'd seen or heard. It was something he'd *sensed*. He looked down at the scarab, then closed his eyes and tightened his grip. He could feel it now, almost like a blip on some internal radar screen, off to his left, getting closer. *Should we go back?* No way.

There was nothing back that way except the side room and, far above now, the crypt. They needed to go deeper, find the Death Walker. He looked up ahead: Ten or fifteen feet in front of them, the tunnel was brighter.

"This way," he said.

As they got closer, he could see that light was spilling into the tunnel from openings on either side. *Side tunnels*, he realized. As they got closer to them, the thing he was sensing got closer, too. *What is it? Is it the Walker?* He didn't think so, but he couldn't say exactly why.

"We need to go faster," he whispered. Whatever it was, they needed to beat it to the intersection. He didn't mention that part, afraid they'd stop instead.

They began hustling down the hallway, their footsteps and breathing getting louder as their pace increased. He looked back: Ren was right behind him. Secure in his speed, Luke loped a little farther back.

"Keep going," breathed Alex, waving for Luke to pick up the pace. Luke waved back: *Hello!*

Alex and Ren zoomed past the side tunnels and stopped. Alex tried to calm down and center himself for another look at that internal radar screen.

But before he could, he saw his cousin just now reaching the intersection. Luke looked to the right and then to the left. And then his eyes grew huge in the green glow. Whatever Alex had sensed was *right there*.

"Oh, snap!" blurted Luke as a pale figure lurched out of the tunnel toward him. It reached for him with outstretched arms, grabbed for him with tightly wrapped fingers.

For one horrible second, Alex thought it had him. But Luke was fast. He went from walking forward to running to the right with one quick swivel of his hips. The mummy charged stiffly after him, and they both disappeared down the passageway.

"LUKE!" Ren screamed.

They both rushed back to the intersection and peered down the passageway. No sign of the mummy or Luke — and ten feet ahead they saw the glow of another intersection.

Alex tried to push the panic out of his mind. They were in a warren of tunnels — and had just lost their strongest member. He closed his hand around the scarab and shut his eyes, trying to focus, trying to find the mummy. Nothing. Already too far away.

Guilt poured into Alex like icy seawater into a sinking boat. On some level, he felt like everything that had happened was because of him. But this was his fault on *every* level. His cousin. Gone. Ren's words echoed in his head, as clear as they'd been that morning. Maybe more so: *"You dragged me there — you served me up!"*

But maybe it wasn't too late to help Luke.

Ren didn't say anything now, just turned with him and ran after Luke. They reached the next passageway. Which way had he gone? They took their best guess and continued on, desperately hoping they'd find him. Hoping there'd be something left to find.

"You can sense them, can't you?" Ren huffed from beside him. "That's why we were running."

"When they're close," Alex gasped.

"How?"

They reached another intersection. Two more choices, the odds stacking against them. They stopped, hands on knees, and Alex considered his answer.

"I don't know," he said. But he did know — he'd sensed that, too. He just wasn't comfortable saying it: *Because they're dead.*

The tunnels twisted and turned. They stopped to investigate another little room, but this one was unfinished, not much more than a cave in the dirt, and there was no sign of Luke. They'd lost him, and now they were lost, too.

"Wait, I . . ." Alex whispered, coming to a sudden halt.

"What is it?" said Ren. She shot a few skittish looks around the empty passageway and then down at the amulet. "Another mummy?"

"I don't know," said Alex, closing his eyes to concentrate. "Feels different."

"Different how?"

He shook his head. This ability was still new to him. "Just different."

Suddenly, his eyes snapped open. He looked directly at Ren. "It's coming this way!"

"Should we run?" said Ren in an urgent whisper.

Alex considered it, and then: "No. We have to stop running. We came here for a reason."

Ren looked up at him. "I was afraid you were going to say that, but . . ."

"But what?" he said urgently.

"But we need to be smart this time. We can't just stand out here and wait to be seen."

Alex knew she was right. If this was the showdown he'd been looking for, they needed to get the upper hand. "The little room," he said.

"An ambush?" she said skeptically. "But what if it's . . ."

But Alex was already rushing back to the little room. "Hurry," he said.

They ducked into the dark, dank chamber. It wasn't much bigger than they were, so all they could do was huddle together inside.

Ren stared out into the soft glow of the hallway and raised the shovel, her hands trembling slightly on the handle.

Alex closed his eyes and gripped the amulet hard. It felt like this thing was right on top of them.

"I don't know . . ." Ren whispered. "If it's *him* . . . I don't know if I can go through that again. This place . . . it's like our own grave."

They heard a noise in the passageway and fell silent. All Alex heard was the blood pounding in his ears, and then . . .

Another noise, closer now, just outside the entrance. Ren raised her shovel a few inches higher, almost scraping the dirt roof. Alex grasped his amulet tighter, the wings of the scarab digging into the soft flesh of his palm. *Had they prepared an ambush — or trapped themselves?*

Too late. It was here.

"Mmrack?"

Such a strange noise . . .

Louder, closer: "Maa-RACK?"

The sound bounced off the walls, and Alex realized that the thing was turning the corner. It was coming inside! Fear and anticipation swirled in his system. Beside him, Ren leaned back until her shoulders hit dirt. Alex took half a step forward to take her place. His eyes burned, but he didn't dare blink.

And there it was.

He couldn't believe it.

A shadow filled the doorway — but only the first foot or so.

"Mm-Rack?" went the mummy cat. "Mma-Raack?"

Alex now knew what happened to meows when they died.

"It's Pai . . ." said Ren, lowering her shovel.

"How did she . . . Where did she . . ." mumbled Alex, baffled.

Her nerves shot, Ren crumbled to the floor, dropping her shovel with a thud. "I'm just glad it's her," she managed. Legs out and back to the wall, she reached one trembling hand toward the creature but reconsidered and drew it back. "Hi, Pai," she whispered.

The thin, half-wrapped cat stood there for a moment, considering them. Then she took a few very deliberate steps toward Ren. She shook her slender frame, flicked one paw against her ragged wrappings, and watched as a pale white object tumbled free, dragging a thin silver chain with it.

"No way," said Ren, her slumped body straightening slightly.

The cat took a four-footed step back and looked up at Ren.

Ren's eyes, frozen with fear a moment earlier, shone brightly as she stared down at it.

"Pick it up," said Alex, his voice rising in the excitement. "It's for you!"

Ren reached down and picked up the amulet.

Her amulet.

It was such a big gift, but such a strange one. Ren's expression was a perfect mix of Christmas morning and Halloween night.

She glanced over at her oldest friend and then back down at her newest. But Pai-en-Inmar was already leaving.

"Wait," said Ren, but living or dead, cats never listened to things like that.

As Pai's bony tail disappeared back into the passageway, Ren lifted the amulet up into the light. She pulled her legs underneath her and used her free hand to push herself up. She stood up stronger this time, straighter. "A bird," she said.

"An ibis," said Alex. "It's a symbol of Thoth, the god of wisdom and writing."

"Thoth?" mumbled Ren. "But why did she . . . I mean, why me?"

Alex looked at the spot where the ancient cat had been. "I think she was paying you back for setting her free."

Ren smiled. "I've got an amulet." She slowly draped it over her neck. "Just like you."

She wrapped her left hand around it. Her breath caught and her eyes opened wide.

As Alex watched, Ren's brown eyes flashed silver.

Ren felt her nerves settle even as her pulse revved. It was a sensation of going very fast under total control. A single image flashed through her mind: a clump of glowing green against a dark background, a distinctive S shape in its center, where the glow was strongest.

The image vanished, and then the afterimage.

Ren released the amulet and took a deep breath.

"What just happened?" said Alex.

"I saw something," said Ren, a note of wonder in her voice. She looked down at the ibis. "It showed me something."

"What?" said Alex. "What did you see?"

And that was the question. What had she seen? It wasn't a memory, and it wasn't imagination. It was something she had never seen before but that she knew, immediately and instinctively, to be true.

She stepped out into the passageway and looked up at the ceiling, one way, and then the other. And there it was, in the glow coming from the top passage, the distinctive S shape she'd just seen, a bright bending line against the softly glowing background.

She looked over at Alex and then down at the ibis. Given to her by a cat cadaver . . . Entirely, alarmingly unwashed . . . But it had given her the one thing she needed most, the one thing that put her most at ease. It had given her knowledge.

"I think I know which way to go," she said.

"You think?" said Alex, his voice skeptical.

"I know," she said.

As she led Alex through the dark, dangerous tunnels, she allowed herself a moment to think about it. She had always had one very simple problem with magic: It didn't make any sense. Wisdom, on the other hand, was right up her alley. The images felt like puzzles for her to decipher.

She wasn't sure, though. As much as she liked knowing the answers, this felt too easy. It was the opposite of extra credit: just given to her. And it was creepy and unnerving to have this thing in her head. It felt like an alien had snuck into her brain and was flipping through the channels. An alien . . . or a ghost.

Her eyes flashed again as she and Alex slipped past another dark, unfinished room. "Okay," she said, and they paused as she worked out the new image.

Two glowing circles, breaking the surface of still, black water.

She realized too late that they were eyes.

Ambush Predator

PUHHHHH!

A massive force struck Alex so hard that he flew sideways into the wall.

This stretch was mostly clay, and he left an Alex-shaped impression in it as he slumped down to the floor. A soft sifting of dirt rained down from the ceiling.

"Alex!" called Ren.

She spun around to find the long iron snout of a crocodile mask turned toward her like the barrel of a gun. Black eyes glistened in the green light. Her hands wrestled futilely with an unseen force clamping down hard on her throat, cutting off the blood flow. In a few seconds, she was dizzy; in a few more, out cold.

Ta-mesah stood there considering his prey.

Clinging to the edge of consciousness, Alex became aware of a faint shuffling sound. Two mummies appeared, the wrappings doing little to disguise the lanky bodies of two formerly healthy teen boys. The nearest one grabbed him, and he could do nothing more than clumsily slap at its arms as it dragged him into the side room. Then his hands were bound with coarse rope and he couldn't even do that.

Ta-mesah relit the room's candles with the wave of his hand.

Alex's head slowly cleared and the world came into view: a small living chamber. There was a simple bed in one corner. Across from it was a tall stone altar with two raised columns framing a vertical indentation. A false door, Alex knew, the gateway between the world of the living and the world of the dead that all Egyptian tombs had. The mummies stood rigidly, blocking the doorway.

Alex was propped up against the wall by the entrance, the flashlights in his pack digging into his lower back. Ren was next to him, her head drooping onto his shoulder. He jostled her with a gentle shrug. "Huh?" she said blearily.

"Wake up, Ren," he said, trying to control his fear. "We're in trouble."

"Trouble?" she mumbled, and then she remembered. Her eyes snapped open and suddenly she was throwing her arms from side to side, struggling against the ropes at her wrists.

"Don't bother," said Ta-mesah.

She froze and looked up.

"Oh no," she said, her shoulders slumping. "Another one."

Alex's battered ribs told him the same thing: that this was another powerful Order operative, like the hyena-masked psychopath they'd faced in New York. "What do you want?" he said defiantly.

"Watch your tongue, boy," said Ta-mesah, "or I'll cut it out."

"I've heard that before," said Alex, remembering similar words falling from the Stung Man's lips. "Didn't end too well for that guy."

"Who says it's over for him?" Ta-mesah's voice echoed slightly through the iron and emerged barely human.

"I banished him," said Alex.

"Is that what you think?"

"That's what I know —"

Ta-mesah flicked his hand and a wave of force smashed into Alex, snapping his upper body back against the plaster wall and knocking the wind from his lungs.

"I can hear the fight in your voice," said Ta-mesah. "But this fight is over. You've lost. Now you will answer my questions."

Alex glared at him. "Why should I? I don't care what you do to me."

"I believe that," said Ta-mesah. "And you've already died once. You've seen the worst. Alive when so many others have died." He smiled. "The doctor, of course."

Alex stiffened, raising his head as Ren lowered hers. "Oh yes," said Ta-mesah, "she is quite dead."

Alex took another quick look at the mummies. Ta-mesah followed his eyes. "No, not her. She served a different purpose."

Alex understood. He knew as well as anyone that the Walkers needed to feed.

"Scumbag," he said.

Ta-mesah ignored him. "I have two questions for you," he said. "And I will ask them only once —"

"I'm not afraid of you."

"Maybe not. But your friend . . ."

Alex looked quickly over at Ren and saw the fear fill her eyes. "Leave her alone!" he shouted.

A soft chuckle echoed through the iron mask. "She has been much quieter than you, no? Because she's smarter." His tone hardened; his voice grew louder. "You will talk or she will die."

Ren gasped with pain and surprise as her bound hands were yanked over her head by an unseen force.

"Stop it!" Alex shouted, but as he watched, she was dragged up the wall. She struggled to get her feet underneath her.

"First question . . ."

"No," said Alex, unable to hide the desperation in his voice.

Ren was standing bolt upright now, her arms straight over her head, but still the invisible force pulled on her hands. She rose to her tiptoes . . .

"Where is your mother, little boy?"

Alex's head snapped back toward his interrogator. "What?" he said, confusion flooding his mind. "*You* have my mom!" he shouted. *Is this some cruel trick?*

"Don't toy with me. I *will* kill the girl!"

Ren's feet left the floor. She groaned in pain as her shoulders took all her weight.

"She must be in the Black Land," shouted Ta-mesah. "Tell us where!"

Alex couldn't believe what he was hearing. The Black Land was Egypt, named for the fertile soil along the Nile. It made no sense.

"I don't know!" screamed Alex. "Leave her alone!"

He reached up for his amulet but could only paw at it with the rope of his heavily tied hands. Ren's feet were a foot off the ground. Alex watched in helpless horror as her shoulders and arms strained. Her face was a mask of pain and despair. She opened her mouth and screamed.

It was a ragged cry, broken only when she gulped for more breath, but in the brief pause, a new sound filled the room.

"Mma-RACK?"

Standing in between the two rigid mummies was a third, much smaller one. The little cat looked from the girl hanging in the air to the man in the mask. In the narrow gaps between the wrappings on her back, what was left of her hair stood on end. She opened her mouth and released a dry, angry *HISS!*

"What is that . . . thing?" said Ta-mesah. His concentration broken, Ren dropped to the ground, landing in a limp crouch.

Pai hissed again, gathered her haunches underneath her, and jumped. She covered the twelve feet to her adversary in one impressive leap. Ta-mesah put his hands up, but it was too late. He got a Pai in the face. He stumbled backward and smacked into the wall, then reached up and frantically attempted to pry the hissing whirlwind from his head.

Pai swiped down repeatedly, her bony front paws landing like turbocharged drumsticks on the iron mask: *TLAK! PRANG!*

"Help me, you idiots!" Ta-mesah called.

The mummies sprang into action, rushing toward the epic hissy fit. Alex and Ren suddenly found themselves in front of the unguarded doorway. "Let's go!" urged Alex.

"We need to help Pai!" countered Ren.

A tightly wrapped arm — *an arm!* — flew past them end-over-end and out into the tunnel.

"I don't think so!" said Alex.

They took one last look back into the candlelit room. Pai was still pummeling Ta-mesah's head, while one mummy struggled to get ahold of the squirming feline and the other gaped down dumbly at the place where its arm had been.

"Thanks, Pai!" Ren called as the friends rushed out of the room, a wave of gratitude briefly washing away her fear. "You rock!"

Hands still tied, amulets bouncing at their necks, they barreled down the tunnel.

They ducked around the next corner. Alex turned around so Ren could fish a small Swiss Army knife out of his backpack. Then she opened it with her teeth and sawed away Alex's ropes. Once free, he returned the favor.

If there was ever a time for action, this was it, but for a long moment Alex just stood there, gawping down at the dirt. He couldn't believe The Order didn't have his mother. All this time . . . Every decision he'd made . . . Were they playing with him? Or was it true?

"Alex!" said Ren, drawing it out so that it sounded like two names: *Al, Lex.*

He shook it off — literally — shaking his head hard and forcing himself to focus. "Okay," he said. "Which way? Use the amulet."

"Nuh-uh," she said. "That thing almost got us killed. It led us right into that trap."

Alex gaped at her. He was focused now. "That's not its fault!"

"What is it, mine?"

"No, but . . ."

"Whatever, I never would've been that dumb without it. Just standing there. I'm done with seeing things — that's what *crazy people* do, Alex."

Alex stared at her. He was sure anything he said now would just make her more determined. He knew how rational she was.

"Anyway," she said, "unless we want to go back, there's only one way left."

Alex definitely didn't want to go back. "Okay," he said. "Let's go."

As they hustled forward, Alex reached into his backpack and unzipped a little compartment built to hold books. He touched the edge of the folder inside, just to confirm that the spell was still there. It was time to cut the head off the snake.

They turned another corner and a brightly lit doorway came into view. "I think that's it," said Ren. "The center of the tomb."

"The tomb chapel," said Alex.

"Sure," said Ren. "That, too."

Alex wrapped his hand around his amulet and his internal radar lit up with a signal so strong it could only be one thing: Captain Willoughby.

They crept closer, Ren's hands balled into fists at her sides, far from her ibis amulet. They moved carefully, even though so far this tomb had none of the scorpions, pits, and blades they'd encountered in New York.

But there were other perils.

A single word greeted them as they crossed the threshold. The sounds were stretched and torn but clear enough: "Welcome."

The Inner Sanctum

Willoughby was standing near the back wall, and there was a young boy tied to a stone slab in front of him.

The boy turned his tear-streaked face toward them. He screamed for help, but a filthy rag tied over his mouth muffled the words. All around him, the walls of the inner sanctum were decorated with the Crown Jewels of Willoughby's native land. The gold and gems reflected the powerful glow of a massive crystal chandelier, lit by something other than electricity.

"It's that boy," said Ren. The hair, the eyes, the slightly lopsided eyebrows . . . "It's Robbie."

Willoughby said something, but the sentence ran together in a thick jangle of internal damage. All Alex caught was the word *escape* and the gravelly chuckle that punctuated it. *The boy tried to escape*, he realized. *And failed.*

Losing interest in the one-sided conversation, the Death Walker turned back to the boy. He was ignoring the friends, unconcerned, and the dismissal angered Alex. Willoughby reached down with one huge hand and picked up a long bronze hook.

Everyone understood that.

The boy screamed through the rag, and Alex went to work.

His left hand on his scarab, his right hand shot forward, fingers pressed tightly together. The lance of wind struck Willoughby's hand, knocking the hook free and sending it flying into the back wall, where it stuck like an arrow.

Willoughby roared his disapproval.

"Do it now," said Ren. "Before he opens his mouth again."

Alex knew it wasn't his ravaged, repulsive words that bothered her. It was the possibility of facing that soul-sucking black abyss again. There'd be no place to hide down here. He swung the pack off his back and reached in for the folder. Before he could pull it free, a powerful force struck him on the shoulder and spun him to the floor.

The backpack went flying. Alex heard it land — the clinks and clunks of loose flashlights — and tried to stand. His shoulder throbbed as he put his hand down for balance.

Across the room, Willoughby stepped out from behind the stone slab. His hand was still pointed in Alex's direction, beefy fingers pressed tightly together.

Alex got to his feet. "I have your attention now, don't I?" he said.

"Wait," called Ren. "Think!"

But Alex's hand had already shot forward again, and Willoughby's hand rose to match him.

Alex's lance of wind met Willoughby's bolt of force, and an invisible battle of wills began in the center of the room. The crystal chandelier tinkled and swayed above them, but Alex could barely hear it over his pounding pulse. He stared into Willoughby's black eyes and clenched his teeth.

Alex's pulse raced dangerously and his head pounded, but he was gratified to hear the Walker's raspy breathing deepen with the effort, like an old man clearing his throat of sand.

He saw some movement in his peripheral vision — a flash of blue, the color of Ren's shirt — but didn't dare break his concentration to see what she was up to.

But the Walker was more powerful and the tide began to turn. Wind began whipping back into Alex's face. His hair blew back as if he were sticking his head out a car window. He tried harder, clenched his fingers tighter, grimaced with effort.

It didn't matter.

A small, wicked smile appeared on the Walker's face, and a moment later his force overwhelmed Alex's wind spear. Alex was spun around and landed heavily on the floor. He added a knee and the other arm to his list of injuries, and threw in his throbbing head as a bonus. But it was Willoughby who got the biggest surprise.

"What'd you do?" he rasped.

Alex looked up. Ren had taken advantage of the standoff to untie the boy. Now they were both rushing toward him, Ren with the backpack in her hands, and the boy reaching up to untie the cloth around his mouth. His first words: "We've got to get out of here!"

"We can't," said Ren, dropping the pack in front of Alex. "There's something we have to do first."

Alex reached in and retrieved the folder. He glanced up at Willoughby, fearing another crushing bolt of force. But the Walker was staring over Alex's shoulder, that same vaguely playful grin on his time-torn face.

Heavy thumps in the hallway. Alex turned in time to see a massive figure thunder into view: 275 pounds and stronger in death than it had been in life. The creature was tightly wrapped and vaguely familiar. Liam's mortal remains filled the entryway and kept coming.

The Other Amulet

The mummy rushed toward Alex and Ren, but Robbie got in the way. "Hey, mummy! You big dummy!" he called.

"Careful!" hissed Ren, but the mummy had already turned toward the boy. He paused for a second. Did he recognize the small, nimble hands that had helped create him? If so, it wasn't a pleasant memory. A harsh, hoarse roar rose from the back of his throat.

The mummy chased Robbie along the wall toward the back of the room as the Death Walker advanced toward Alex and Ren. He used short words and drew them out. He wanted them to understand their fate: "One will die," he said. "One will be my new" — and though the last word was longer and the S's could just as easily have come from a python, it was understandable, too — "asssiissstannt."

Ren's reply was directed not at him, but at Alex. "Now!" she called.

Alex shook the tattered spell free and let the folder fall to the ground.

170

Willoughby stopped in his tracks. Even a bad archaeologist can recognize the Book of the Dead.

But there was no fear in the Walker's expression, only cold appraisal. Meanwhile, Alex's hands trembled as he lifted the ancient text, threatening to tear the dry, fragile fabric.

"He's too close," said Ren.

Alex knew she was right. Willoughby was barely ten feet away now, and capable of striking from a distance. Alex wouldn't be able to read three lines before the Walker knocked him flat or drained his soul.

"Heads up!" called Robbie.

He'd led the mummy around the stone slab and taken a sharp turn back toward the front of the room. He was heading right toward Willoughby. A few lumbering steps behind him, so was Liam.

"Genius," murmured Alex.

Ren reached over and took the spell. "Do it," she said.

All at once:

Willoughby turned toward the onrushing commotion.

Robbie, just a few feet from his former boss, executed a nifty soccer-field fake. He cut left and then darted off to the right.

The mummy barreled on straight ahead, as mummies do.

Alex grasped his amulet, raised his hand, and released the most powerful lance of wind yet — not at the Walker's body, but at the mummy's feet.

The mummy toppled forward at full speed and wiped Willoughby out like all ten bowling pins. It landed on top of its master, their long limbs tangled in the dirt.

Meanwhile, Alex had already begun the recitation. The letters on the tattered text began to glow as he clutched his amulet. This was the scarab's most formidable power: activating the Book of the Dead. The question now: Did he have the right spell? "For Protection Against Grave Robbers and Outland Thieves . . ." There would be no protection for them if he was wrong.

Still, the amulet gave him focus and steadied his hands as he began to recite the opening. The words were familiar, though the sounds were ancient: "O thief! O usurper! Get back! Return, for you should know justice . . ." He heard a loud thump as Willoughby pushed himself free. Alex pressed on: *halfway done.* He heard slurred, ragged speech, unknowable profanities as Willoughby struggled to climb to his feet. *Three quarters.*

"It's working!" said Ren. "He can barely move."

The light above them faded and the symbols on the scroll glowed all the brighter. Alex read the final words.

Done.

He looked up, expecting to find the Walker turned to a dried-out corpse, the way the Stung Man had been. Instead, he saw Willoughby down on the floor, one knee up and one knee down. The Death Walker shook his head, as if to clear some cobwebs. Then he looked up and rose to his feet. The mummy rose to join him. The chandelier glowed brighter overhead.

"Oh no," said Ren, her voice soft with defeat.

"But I . . ." said Alex. He had the wrong spell after all. He'd been so sure, and that sureness, that certainty had doomed them all.

"That wasn't good, was it?" said Robbie.

It was Willoughby who answered. Not with words, which had never been his strength, but with brute force. He pulled his hand back and punched the air.

"Ooomph!" went Alex, doubling over from a fierce shot to the gut.

The spell fluttered to the ground nearby. By the time it landed, Willoughby had already used his powers to strike Alex again. He walked forward slowly, taking his time, not even bothering to look at the others. He had decided who to kill first.

Ren felt helpless. Willoughby was going to beat Alex to death, and there was nothing she could do about it. In her desperation, she turned to the only option she had left. She reached up and wrapped her left hand around her amulet. A simple hope took shape. Magic had never made sense to her, but maybe, just maybe, this amulet — her own amulet — could help her make sense of magic. She needed it now.

What she got was another cryptic image: an empty courtroom, oil lamps unlit on the polished wooden tables . . . For a split second she began to puzzle it out: *Didn't Alex say something about Willoughby skipping out on his trial?*

No, no, no, she thought. She needed something more direct than pictures. She raised her right hand, as she'd seen Alex do so many times. She pointed it at Willoughby and jabbed at the air.

Nothing.

The Walker was having more luck. He punched his hand forward again, and Alex's body convulsed hard on the floor. Ren knew he couldn't take much more. She jabbed at the air again.

Useless.

What good are you? she thought. As if in answer, her eyes flashed silver again. Another image. A man's arm, a block of wood . . .

Robbie shouted something at her and then ducked off to the side, but none of that registered. She was too far inside her own head now. She didn't even notice as the mummy lumbered past her and took up its position.

Another image: an ax. Suddenly, the pieces clicked into place. Alex had *definitely* said something about that. "Still gross," she whispered.

She scanned the room and did a quick inventory:

Alex barely alive, a hulking mummy blocking the doorway, and Robbie crouched down along the far wall —

"I need your help!" she called.

Alex rolled over onto his back and coughed, sending a searing pain through his battered ribs. He reached up and wiped his mouth, painting a red smear across the back of his hand. He looked up to see Willoughby's cruel, carved features staring down at him. Along the far wall, he saw Ren whispering something to Robbie.

He reached for his amulet, pawing at his chest a few times before finding it. He was barely able to close his hand around it, and when he raised the other one, all he could manage was a gentle puff of wind. The scarab slid free to the sound of Willoughby's grisly laughter.

He would die here. He would die without ever finding his mom. Above him, Willoughby pulled back his hand. One more phantom punch, one more wave of force . . . They both knew that would do it.

So did Ren. "Stop it!" she screamed. She threw herself down to the floor in front of Alex and turned to face Willoughby. "If you kill us both, you won't have a new servant!"

"I can be your servant," came a voice. "I was dumb. I won't try to escape again."

"Robbie!" screamed Ren. "You snake!"

"Sorry, but I don't even know you," he said with a shrug. "And I want to live."

Ren glared at him. Alex would have, too, but he could barely lift his head.

"I can help with these two," said Robbie. He raised a large pair of razor-sharp metal shears.

Peering over Ren's shoulder, Alex thought they looked like the nastiest pair of hedge clippers he'd ever seen.

Willoughby smiled down at his once and future assistant, the way one might upon finding a lost five-dollar bill in a coat pocket.

Meanwhile, Alex and Ren were having an exchange of their own.

"Watch out," she whispered to him over her shoulder. "This could get messy."

"What?" said Alex, barely able to form the word.

"I think I know why the spell didn't work. It's because he's a thief and needs to be punished here in this world before he can be judged in the next one."

Alex didn't ask her how she knew. He didn't have the breath for it. But based on what he knew of ancient Egyptian justice, it made immediate sense. "Of course," he managed. "But the punishment for stealing . . ."

Ren nodded and turned back toward the Death Walker. Willoughby drew his fist back farther this time, preparing to unleash a force wave strong enough to crush both friends. He pulled his hand all the way behind his back.

"The punishment . . ." Ren began.

SSNNNIIPPP!

The metal shears snapped shut, making a grotesque sound as they cut through muscle and old bone. Robbie squeezed with every muscle in his small body — and all the anger in there, too — leaning his chest and all his weight down on the handles.

"The punishment," Ren finished, "is cutting off the thief's hand."

Willoughby's hand dropped to the dirt floor with a dull thud.

Collapse

Losing his hand proved entirely disarming for Willoughby.

He fell to his knees and let out a low groan. In the few moments it took him to look from his betrayer to the doorway, where the massive mummy had just collapsed in a heap, his face had already aged visibly. His unnatural vigor draining from him like the last air from a balloon, his big frame slumped. His ravaged windpipe released one last ragged gasp of protest before falling mercifully silent.

"You read the right spell," said Ren, a smile blossoming on her face as she turned back toward Alex. "Cutting off the hand was the only thing left."

A grisly tableau of life and death played out in fast-forward in front of them. Willoughby's blank eyes slipped closed and his wrinkled skin grew tight and leathery and dry. His big frame tightened and pitched forward. Muscle collapsed in on itself until all that was left was skin and bone, facedown on the floor in an old explorer's outfit. The friends watched in fascination and horror — and no small amount of satisfaction — until a clang drew their eyes away.

Robbie had dropped the shears and now ran over to join the others.

"You did it!" chirped Ren.

"That was disgusting!" said Robbie. "And I've seen disgusting down here."

Alex finally realized what the two had been whispering about along the far wall. "Nice acting," he managed.

He turned toward Ren and really looked at her for the first time in days: a little girl in a blue shirt and jeans with dirt on her face. While all he could think to do was attack, she'd done what she did best — and saved him. He gathered up as much air as his bruised lungs would hold.

"You make the best plans," he managed.

She flashed him a quick smile. "I know," she said, and then her smile turned mischievous. "You should try it sometime."

Alex nodded, glad he'd get the chance. Then they heard a ripple of noise from Willoughby's crumpled corpse and turned to look. The body was motionless, except for the stump where its hand had been, which had begun pumping a steady stream of red liquid into the room. No one had to wonder what it was this time. The chandelier began to fade to black as the floor near the body began to turn red.

"Gross," said Ren.

A small tremor shook the room.

"I think we need to get out of here," said Alex.

The other two helped him up. Alex winced from the pain in his ribs and gut.

Ren emptied the three lights from the backpack and stuck the ancient spell back inside. She looked around the room in the failing light. "The Crown Jewels," she said.

"Yes," said Alex.

A larger tremor nearly knocked them all down, but they were both museum kids, and they wouldn't leave such priceless pieces behind. Robbie and Ren raced around, plucking the jewels from the wall and stuffing them in Alex's pack. Ren wrestled a heavy purple crown ringed with a galaxy of multicolored jewels from its perch as Robbie grabbed a scepter topped with a diamond the size of a baby's fist.

"Hurry," said Alex, training his flashlight beam on the ceiling. Like the rest of the underground labyrinth, it had no supports, no crossbeams, and Alex now understood that the force holding it all up was the same thing that had been keeping it lit: Willoughby. Alex shone his flashlight back that way. The flow of dark liquid had intensified and was beginning to pool around the body.

Suddenly, the entire room shuddered and shifted. Dirt and clay rained down in chunks from the ceiling and the plaster on the walls began to crack loudly.

"This whole thing is going to come down!" shouted Ren.

They got out fast. Ren and Robbie helped Alex over the Liam-shaped lump at the entrance. The tomb where the mummies were created would now be their grave. The tunnel was pitch-dark, the green glow gone. They pointed their flashlights straight ahead.

"I'm okay," said Alex. Adrenaline was flooding his system, and if he bent over at just the right angle, he could manage a decent jog. "I'll follow as fast as I can."

They both shook their heads, and Alex was in no condition to argue. He pushed harder, ignoring the pain. All he could do now was hope it was fast enough to stay ahead of the crumbling walls. The air in the tunnels filled with a sickening coppery smell — the scent of Willoughby's blood.

"This way!" said Ren, one hand wrapped around her amulet. Reservations or not, this was no time for wrong turns.

A voice called out from the next intersection. "Is that you guys?"

Alex and Ren leveled their flashlights to be sure: Luke!

Alex couldn't manage more than a smile, but Ren called out: "Where were you? Are you okay?"

"That stupid thing was chasing me," said Luke as they caught up with him. "Then it just keeled over!"

"You've been running this *whole time*?" said Ren as the flashlights revealed large sweat stains on his T-shirt.

Luke shrugged. "Probably only four, five miles. We were going in kind of a loop."

"Alex is hurt," said Ren. "Help him, okay?"

"Sure." Luke nodded toward Robbie as he wrapped a strong arm around Alex. "Some people are looking for you," he said.

They hustled up the dark tunnel. There was no sign of Ta-mesah on the way up, his chamber off in a collapsing side tunnel, and the outcome of the catfight unclear. But there were other dangers. Lumps of dirt and clay continued to peel off and fall from the walls and ceiling around them.

"We need to hurry," said Ren.

The fear of being buried alive beneath the old cemetery was on all of their minds. But none of them, not even Robbie, rushed on ahead. They would all make it out, or none of them would.

They were close now.

A two-foot chunk of dirt and stone broke loose from the top of the tunnel and landed with a thud in front of them. They had to scramble around it, and hope the next one wouldn't land on their heads or bring the whole tunnel down. A deep rumble rose up behind them as the entire system began to collapse. Dirt and mud and clay were everywhere: raining down from above and rising up from below.

"We're not going to make it!" yelped Robbie.

But Alex couldn't accept that. After relying on only himself this entire time, after pushing relentlessly forward without really caring who came along, he realized something. Every single one of these people had saved his life. Now it was his turn.

"Yes, we are," he said. His head hurt as much as his ribs, but he reached up and wrapped his hand around his amulet. He envisioned a perfect, round tunnel in front of them and pushed his hand forward, fingers spread, to make it so.

Eyes closed, teeth clenched, Alex gave it everything he had left.

His feet moved mechanically forward, and he went where Luke led. With all his strength, he used his amulet to create a wind tunnel around them. He could only hope the outward pressure would be enough to keep the walls and ceiling from collapsing in and burying them alive.

He was on the edge of unconsciousness, his strength spent, when he felt the wind blast back at him. His eyes edged open to reveal the stone door at the back of the crypt, slid halfway open to the Highgate night beyond.

Next Steps

The taxi pulled up at the Campbell, and they all pooled their money to pay the man. Ren unlocked the main door with the skeleton key, and they stumbled inside. Alex limped in last, all but drooling at the thought of the aspirin in his room. He was kind of looking forward to seeing Somers's wrinkly old face, too. But that wasn't the face that greeted them.

"Hello, children," he heard.

He immediately recognized the crisp German accent. Alex looked up and there he was: Todtman, smiling his froggy smile and leaning on a sleek black cane.

"Boy, am I glad to see you," said Ren, rushing up and giving him a hug.

Alex wasn't rushing anywhere at the moment, but he gave his old mentor the biggest smile he could muster — and the biggest news he could imagine: "They don't have my mom!"

A few minutes later, they were scattered around the little reception area of the closed museum: Alex and Ren on a battered old couch, Todtman on a wooden chair across from them, Robbie standing by the door, and Luke stretching on the floor, "post-workout." Alex did most of the talking, slowly and carefully telling Todtman what they'd found.

When he was done, he sat back and tried to catch up on his breathing. His injured ribs made it hard to take deep breaths, so he had to make do with short, shallow ones.

"The Black Land?" repeated Todtman. His leg was stretched out in front of him, as straight as his new cane.

As Alex gathered his breath to respond, he glanced at the jet-black walking stick: a lasting souvenir of their battle with the Stung Man. These battles were taking a toll. But now, at last, he felt like they were making progress. "They think she's in Egypt," he said, before repeating his top story. "They don't have her!"

He broke into a smile, despite his aches and pains.

"But where is she, then?" said Ren. "If she's not a prisoner, if they're looking for her, too . . ."

Todtman said what they were all thinking: "Why would she hide from us?"

The smile faded from Alex's face. *Why would she hide from me?* "She must have a good reason," he said. "She wouldn't just —" His eyes got wide and he swung toward Ren. "Use your thing! Ask it!"

"It's not a Magic 8 Ball, Alex," she said, glancing down at the ibis. And then, quieter: "And anyway, I already did. No response."

"Are you sure you're using it right?" he said, his voice more accusatory than he'd intended.

"I'm not sure *I'm* using *it* at all!" she said, her voice more defensive than she'd intended. "I think it might be the other way around."

Alex backed off. "Okay, sorry," he said. "I just thought, maybe . . ."

Ren relented, too. "I know," she said softly.

Alex looked at her. She was still his best friend. They'd had a fight, they'd failed each other and put each other in danger, but they'd also bailed each other out. Their friendship had changed in some way that he couldn't quite wrap his head around, but he had learned one thing clearly: He couldn't do this without her.

"Ta-mesah — the crocodile guy — said something else, too," said Ren, turning back toward Todtman. "He said we didn't really get rid of the Stung Man. Or that's what it seemed like he was saying, anyway."

Todtman thought briefly before speaking. "I think he might be right. I've been thinking about it. The Book of the Dead and the scarab can send the Death Walkers back to the afterlife . . . but that's where they just came from —"

Alex got it now. "They could cling to the edge between life and death again, avoiding final judgment."

"And waiting for another chance to escape," finished Todtman. "In fact, they might even be stronger now, recharged by their time in this world."

"You're kidding me," said Ren. "You mean they could come back?"

"They must be judged. They need to go through the weighing of the heart ceremony. That is what they fear. They know their hearts would be found to be full of guilt, and instead of entering the afterlife, they'd be lost forever."

"But how do we do that?" Ren began.

"The Lost Spells," said Alex.

"Precisely," said Todtman. "It was the Lost Spells that brought them back. They are more powerful than the known spells, and the last one, I believe, deals directly with the weighing of the heart. I think that may be what this is all about."

Somers ambled into the room with a fresh ice pack for Alex.

"Thanks, Somers," he said.

The old caretaker had sat through Alex's recap, right up until the part where Dr. Aditi's fate was confirmed. Then he'd gotten up and left the room. He was too old for grand quests. His part was done.

Alex handed Somers the melted pack and pressed the new one to his side. A shiver went through him. "There's a lot I still don't understand," he said, leaning back into the couch. "Like why did Willoughby look like his statue and not his photo?"

Todtman considered it. "The ancient Egyptians had those statues made because they believed they could inhabit the images in the afterlife," he said. "Tell me, on the way out of the crypt, did the statue still have its hand?"

"I was too out of it to notice," said Alex.

"I didn't check," said Ren. "It was dark."

They all looked over at Luke. He had both legs stretched out in front of him and was reaching down and grabbing his sneakers. "Don't look at me," he said without looking up. "I was out the door in about point-four seconds."

A few quick knocks drifted in from the next room. Someone was at the front door, and there was a muffled exchange of voices as Somers let them in.

"They're here!" cried Robbie, rushing out of the room.

Alex looked over and saw Ren take one last look at the flyer in her lap before folding it in half. Of course she'd kept the thing.

Luke sprang to his feet. "Family reunion time," he said. "You guys coming?"

But he was already gone, after a reward or just a happy ending.

Alex and Todtman labored to stand, and Ren waited politely for them.

"We're going to Egypt, aren't we?" said Alex, once they were all up.

"Of course," said Todtman. "All those questions you still have. I am sure the answers are to be found in the Black Land."

"The answers, and my mom," said Alex.

"And the Lost Spells," said Ren.

"And another Death Walker," said Todtman. "Maybe more than one."

The three joined Luke in the next room. There was the old couple, with wraparound smiles on their faces and eyes full of tears. And those eyes were on a lovely woman with light brown hair and one eyebrow just slightly higher than the other, currently hugging the heck out of her son.

The others hung back a bit, giving Robbie and his family a little space.

"They're getting stronger," said Ren. "The Death Walkers are getting stronger."

Alex was mesmerized by the sight of the mother-and-son reunion, but he finally peeled his eyes away when Ren spoke. He knew she was right. He'd noticed it, too, but he knew something else. He looked around at three amulets and one future Olympian and a tearful reunion that they'd made possible. "The Walkers are getting stronger," he said. "But so are we."

The others nodded and hugged, respectively, and for a few moments, the old museum fell silent. The only sound: the delicate rhythm of small footsteps on the fourth floor.

But Walkers and Keepers and cats were not the only parties involved. And far away from the English night, deep under shifting Egyptian sands, the death cult was making strides of its own.

Night or day made no difference in the ancient headquarters of The Order. A large false door stood in the center of one wall, and it was changing. The red-orange paint covering the vertical gash in its center began to shimmer. A man emerged from the once-solid stone, stepping into the room in one assured stride.

On his head, a heavy iron mask, looking no less fearsome for the rows of fresh, deep scratches.

Another man, in another mask, turned to look.

They didn't bother with pleasantries. "The Englishman has been defeated, for now," said Ta-mesah. "It was the boy again, and there's another. No matter: The portals work."

The gash in the false door turned back to dull stone. The leader nodded, the brutal beak of his Egyptian vulture mask dipping up and down. "The Amulet Keepers can't stop what is coming," he said. "I will tell him that it is all going according to plan."

Don't Miss

TOMBQUEST

BOOK 3
VALLEY OF KINGS

Egypt is in the grip of madness. Voices
in the air whisper dark secrets, and flashes
of light burn across the night sky.

Alex and Ren must travel deep into the
heart of the Egyptian desert, to the
Valley of the Kings. Will they find the
Lost Spells, or will another Death
Walker be lying in wait?

**Each book unlocks traps and treasure
in the TombQuest game!**

Log in now to join the adventure.
Scholastic.com/TombQuest

TOMBQUEST

Enter your code to unlock traps and treasure!

R4RRMFMCX7